THE DISAPPEARANCE OF EMILY H.

Also by Barrie Summy

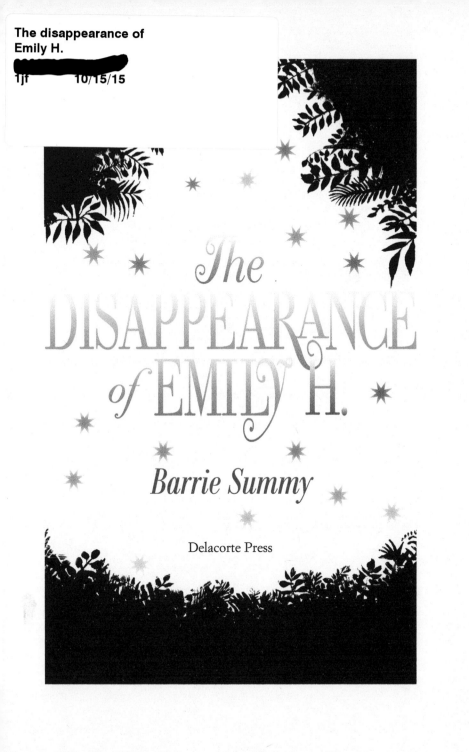

The
DISAPPEARANCE
of EMILY H.

Barrie Summy

Delacorte Press

Text copyright © 2015 by Barbara Summy
Jacket art copyright © 2015 by Jeffrey Fisher

All rights reserved. Published in the United States by Delacorte Press,
an imprint of Random House Children's Books, a division of Random House LLC,
a Penguin Random House Company, New York.

Delacorte Press is a registered trademark and the colophon is a trademark of
Random House LLC.

randomhousekids.com

Educators and librarians, for a variety of teaching tools, visit us at
RHTeachersLibrarians.com

Library of Congress Cataloging-in-Publication Data
Summy, Barrie.
The disappearance of Emily H. / Barrie Summy. — First edition.
pages   cm
Summary: Eighth-grader Raine, a new girl at Yielding Middle School,
uses her supernatural ability to see other people's memories
to solve the disappearance of a teenaged girl.
ISBN 978-0-385-73943-6 (hc) — ISBN 978-0-385-90790-3 (glb) —
ISBN 978-0-375-89756-6 (ebook)
[1. Mystery and detective stories. 2. Missing children—Fiction. 3. Memory—
Fiction. 4. Supernatural—Fiction. 5. Middle schools—Fiction.
6. Schools—Fiction.] I. Title.
PZ7.S9546Di   2015
[Fic]—dc23   2014034338

The text of this book is set in 12-point Simoncini Garamond font.
Book design by Trish Parcell

Printed in the United States of America
10 9 8 7 6 5 4 3 2 1
First Edition

For Rachel Vater Coyne:
in this busy, noisy world,
I'm so grateful our paths crossed.

CHAPTER 1

For once I'd like to go to a school with a really unique mascot. Like a garden gnome. Or a three-toed sloth. Or a geoduck.

Instead, I'm going to Yielding Middle.

From across the street I stare at its boring red bricks and horizontal stripes of windows. But mostly I notice the faded mural above the front doors. It's of a scruffy cougar pouncing on a football. This is my fourth cat school.

Eighth grade officially starts next week, but today is registration. My stomach is heavy, like I ate stones for lunch instead of strawberry Pop-Tarts.

A couple of guys are on the front lawn, winging a Frisbee back and forth past the flagpole. One guy has spiked red hair and looks like the flagpole's twin: tall and freakishly thin. The other guy's closer to average height and weight, with wild brown hair and a baggy T-shirt and jeans. He might even be cute, but I'm not close enough to tell. Students passing by heckle them about their lousy throws and yell at them to come in and get their pictures taken.

Everyone's in groups or at least pairs, laughing and joking as they disappear around the corner to where registration's happening. It's only new kids like me who arrive solo and silent.

I reach into my front pocket for the small, scratched-up silver heart with a dent in the side where I once dropped it on the sidewalk. I balance the heart in my palm and watch as tiny sparkles dance across it, sparkles only I can see.

I need a memory from my first day of kindergarten. A shot of courage for facing Yielding Middle and all the yuck that goes along with being the new girl.

I close my hand to trap the sparkles, then shut my eyes, drifting into the memory.

The small kitchen smells of coffee and maple syrup. My grandmother sits on a wooden chair while I stand in front of her, close enough that she can reach my head with the brush.

"Kindergarten." She divides my hair into three sections and begins braiding from high on my crown.

"I can handle it," I say, chewing a bite of pancake.

"Of course you can." She tugs, getting the braid tight and perfect. "You can already read." Tug. "You can count to one hundred." Tug. "You can print your whole name." Tug.

2

I gulp some milk.

"And look." She pulls a deep blue ribbon from her apron pocket and lays it on the table in front of me. "Brand-new."

My eyes grow big. More new stuff to go along with the school supplies and the lunch box and the shoes? Starting school is better than Christmas.

My grandmother turns me around. Because she's still seated, we're at the same height, and looking into her clear gray eyes is like looking into a mirror.

"Raine," she says, "don't pick up any sparkles at school."

"Not even the really bright ones?"

"Don't touch any of them. People don't understand how we read their memories."

"They don't want to share?"

"You'll fit in better if you leave the sparkles alone." She places her hands on my shoulders and stares at me, unblinking. "Promise me."

I hesitate, biting my bottom lip. "I promise."

"Good girl." She reaches into her apron pocket again, this time pulling out a thin chain with a small, shiny silver heart glimmering with sparkles. She places it in my hand, then gently folds my fingers over it. "Whenever you need to, Raine, you can always look at these."

I close my eyes. My grandmother must've been carrying around the heart for a while. It's jam-packed with memories of us together: playing Go Fish, swinging in the park, baking cupcakes, making Play-Doh snakes.

"Are you okay?" A voice jolts me out of the vision.

I open my eyes, still flooded with a warm, happy feeling, the kind you wish you could hold on to forever, the kind of feeling that makes you think you can take on the world and win.

Standing next to me is a very bright girl. She's wearing a tie-dyed T-shirt dress with swirls of red, orange, and lime-green. Put her in a cone and she'd look like rainbow sherbet. Her dirty-blond hair is obscenely long, past her butt, and as straight as a stick.

"I'm good," I say, sliding the heart back into my pocket.

"I was getting worried. One of my cousins has seizures, and I thought maybe that's what was happening with you. I'm Shirlee, by the way. With two *e*'s." She talks fast. Anxiety is rolling off her in waves. I can practically smell it.

"My name's Raine."

"Raine? That's different."

"It's basically a weather reference. A huge storm was going on the night I was born." So huge, my mother never made it to the hospital, and I was born in a car.

"So you could've been called Thunder or Lightning or Cloud?"

"I got lucky with Raine." Believe me, I've thought of all the possibilities: Pontiac, Backseat, Vinyl.

She squints in the sunlight. "Where do we go to pick up our schedules? And get our pictures taken?"

She must be new, too, which explains why she's so nervous. "The gym?" I say. "I just moved here yesterday." I

4

step off the curb, and she follows, like a puppy in search of a new friend.

"Welcome to Yielding, New York," she says, pushing her hair behind her ear to reveal a dangly metal sun earring with sixteen rays and a wide smile. "Did you hear the sirens last night?"

"Yeah," I say. "What happened?"

"A hay field outside town caught fire. It burned for a while before anyone realized it. On the news this morning, they said it was arson. Fourth fire like that this summer."

Shirlee chats about Yielding. She's one of those people who can handle both sides of a conversation. Works for me.

"This is my first time going to regular school. I've been homeschooled my entire life," she tells me. "What about you?"

"This is my third middle school, my fifth school altogether," I say. "I'm hoping this time's the charm, and I make it the whole way through twelfth grade here." Although I'm not sure I see my mom totally changing her pattern, which goes like this: find a deadbeat guy, get involved, have an ugly breakup, drag daughter off to a new town for a fresh start.

"Five schools?" Shirlee looks shocked, as if I told her I'm from Mars.

My fingers begin to tingle with pins and needles, like I've been sitting on them. There must be a sparkle on her somewhere, but I can't see it. I lift my arms, just a little, reaching toward Shirlee, trying to sense where the sparkle is.

She glances at me.

I drop my arms to my sides. I miss the days when the whole world was brilliant with sparkles, when I could spot them and scoop up people's memories as easily as breathing. That all changed when I was twelve. I woke up one morning and the world was duller, with way fewer sparkles. I have no idea why and no one to ask.

Once Shirlee and I hit school property, we follow the sound of voices and make our way to the gym. Immediately inside the double doors, a couple of overweight women wearing Cougars T-shirts sit behind a table.

The woman on the left takes care of me, getting my name and handing me my schedule. The woman on the right does the same for Shirlee.

"You girls done your photo for your student card yet?" my woman asks.

When we say no, she directs us to room five.

"Come back here after and buy your PE clothes." She jerks a thumb over her shoulder in the direction of the far basketball hoop.

"Let's see what classes we have together." Shirlee reads from her schedule as we walk along the hall.

My fingers are still tingling, but I've given up trying to find the sparkle on her. "Film," I say when Shirlee finishes. "Last period." Only school I've ever gone to with a film class. For the first time since I walked through the double doors with the cougar mascot, a little bit of interest pierces through the general annoyance I feel at my mother for forcing me to change schools again.

"Film? That's it? But we're both in eighth grade." She's incredulous.

"There must be a lot of eighth graders."

We wander the halls, looking for room five.

Eventually, Shirlee flips over her schedule and examines the map on the back. "We took a wrong turn at the restrooms." She taps the middle of the paper.

I nod, looking over her shoulder. "I was expecting to meet you, you know," she says as we retrace our steps.

"What?"

"My horoscope said I was destined to meet a new friend today."

"You're coming to a big public school. You'll meet loads of new people," I say. I don't comment on the word *friend*. With all the moving we've done, I'm not much of a friend maker.

"True," Shirlee says. "But there was also something about height, which I didn't understand at the time. Now I know it was referring to your"—she looks at my head and then my feet—"shortness."

I blink. At five foot one, I'm small, but I won't be the shortest student here. Shirlee's obviously working at making the horoscope thing fit.

Room five's a mob scene, with students in a noisy, messy, zigzaggy line. My fingers tingle so bad it's like they're on fire. I shove my hands in my pockets. Feeling for memories here would be social suicide. Nothing screams *different* louder than reaching for people's backpacks, necklaces, clothes, whatever.

"Next," the photographer announces in a robotic voice. He waits a few seconds, then calls again. "Next."

"Next." In a low, gravelly voice, a girl mimics him to her friend.

"Go in front of me?" Shirlee pulls out a tube of gloss. "I'm the opposite of photogenic. I'm probably related to Medusa." She uncaps the gloss, and a scent of thyme or oregano or some other pizza herb is released into the air. "I bet you never take a bad picture."

"Not true," I say, thinking back to last fall and my zombie-ish seventh-grade photo ID.

"I don't believe it." She studies me as if I'm a bug under a microscope. "You're really pretty. Your hair is full of body. And you've got very unusual eyes." She peers at me. "Gray." She steps back. "I bet you could be a model."

"Next."

A blonde with perfectly styled chin-length hair and a short clingy dress glances over her shoulder at us. She looks me up and down, then stares at Shirlee and slaps her hands over her eyes. "Help. Someone get me sunglasses. That dress is burning into my eyeballs."

The mean girl. Every school has one.

"Eww," several girls mock-scream, also covering their eyes.

The mean girl's accessories. Every school has them, too.

Shirlee freezes, like maybe that'll turn her invisible. Homeschooling didn't prepare her for mean girls.

"Next."

My fingers itch like crazy. A huge sparkle glitters from the blonde's purse. I inch closer to her. Just as I begin to stretch out my arm, a laugh comes from the front of the room.

Like a wave, everyone in line surges forward, craning their neck to see what's going on. The sparkle moves out of reach.

There's another laugh.

It's the two Frisbee guys from the lawn. The brown-haired guy's hanging on to a video controller, making faces and noises, and basically hamming it up for the redheaded guy getting his picture taken.

"He's cute," Shirlee says, her eyes on the brown-haired guy. "That's something you don't see with homeschooling."

Homeschooling would kill me, but not because of the lack of boys. My mom and I could never handle that much together time. Not and be nice to each other.

There's another burst of laughter as the cute guy pulls Ping-Pong balls from his backpack and bounces them off his friend's spiky hair.

While everyone's eyes are glued on the two boys, I slip between people until I'm behind the mean blonde. Three. Two. One. Fast as lightning, I shoot out my arm and grab the sparkle off her purse.

CHAPTER 2

*T*he sparkle tickling my palm, I close my eyes to see the memory.

The blonde opens the door of an old car and slides into the passenger seat. She shakes her head, swinging her hair like she's in a shampoo commercial. She beams at the driver, but her eyes dart nervously around the car. "Hey, Michael."

"What're you doing, Jennifer?" The guy behind the steering wheel frowns. Even with the super irritated look on his face, he's cute, double-take cute, with high cheekbones, clear blue eyes, and broad shoulders.

"I happened to be over here." She swallows.

He turns the key in the ignition.

She jerks the seat belt across her chest and clicks it in, then sits still, like she's hoping to get away with something.

"Seriously?" Every syllable is heavy with annoyance.

"So, uh, how's robotics going?" Her nails dig into her thighs.

"I gotta be somewhere." He nods at the door, as in Get out. *Her face falls.*

He fiddles with the radio, ignoring her.

She presses the button to release her seat belt.

I open my eyes to more laughter. Everyone's still focused on the front of the line. Not on me. I glance down at my palm, watching the sparkle fade.

So the mean girl's name is Jennifer.

I watch her. With one hip jutted way out, Jennifer oozes attitude. She leans over and whispers to her friends. In sync, two of them turn, point at Shirlee, and giggle. A few seconds later, two more girls give Shirlee the same treatment. Then Jennifer looks at her and bursts into a fake laugh.

Hard to believe this is the awkward, tense girl from the car. Who's Michael? He looked older, maybe from high school.

Most of the time, I lift boring, everyday memories. People doing dishes or eating. Or else I pick up snippets of conversation that don't make sense. Often I get nothing. But every once in a while, I get an unexpected gift. A memory that shows someone in a completely different light. Like when the mean girl likes a guy who couldn't care less.

Should I feel bad about hijacking other people's memories? Maybe. But I don't. Some people come from a family with loads of money. Some ace math without trying. Some never get zits. Reading sparkles is my thing, my little talent. I don't spot them on everyone I meet. But when I do see one, I'm grabbing it.

After my photo, I leave Shirlee trying to talk the photographer into taking extra shots of her, and head back to the gym.

I'm at the gym, in line for PE clothes, when she shows up and Velcros herself to me. She's her chatty self again, so by the time we've got our shorts and T-shirts, I know that Shirlee Bruce, no middle name, lives with both parents and has two older sisters away at college. That her mom named Shirlee after her grandmother, a poet and children's librarian. That Shirlee's big-time into her horoscope, the way some people are into checking their messages every two seconds. Somewhere between a hobby and an addiction.

We split up so she can join the Spanish club. I fight my way across the crowded gym to the cross-country sign-ups.

Elbows on the table, Jennifer is talking to the girl on the other side. The mean, popular girl is a runner? Really? She couldn't play volleyball or tennis?

"You finish the summer English assignment yet?" Jennifer asks.

"No, but Danielle said it was hard," the girl replies.

"That whole situation is going to end up sucking for us." Jennifer flicks her wrist impatiently.

"Seriously." The other girl nods slowly and, looking up, catches sight of me. "Oh, hi. You here to sign up for cross-country?"

"Yeah," I say.

"Later," Jennifer says to her friend, and takes off. She doesn't even glance my way.

The girl rummages through a stack of papers on the table. "I'm Alyssa, by the way. Just give me a sec. Torie was manning the table this morning. No one can figure out her system." Still rummaging, Alyssa frowns and mutters, "If she even has a system."

Alyssa's really pretty. Her hair's this unusual tea-brown color with red highlights. It's thick and hangs to just above her shoulders. Her face is perfectly symmetrical, and her eyes match her hair. She's wearing a charm bracelet, and a sparkle glints from a dangling cupcake.

"We've got a good team," she says, switching her attention to the papers in a plastic box. "Made it all the way to state last year."

"Cool." I could get into being part of a competitive team.

"Where are you from?" she asks.

"Detroit."

"I've never been there," she says.

"You're not missing much." My eyes are on the miniature cupcake and its glittering sparkle. My fingers

13

tingle. I'm dying to grab it, but can't see a way to without looking weird.

"So, you run cross-country before?" Alyssa asks.

I nod. "The girl who was ahead of me . . . is she on the team?"

"Jennifer? She's our best."

Sounds like I have a challenge ahead of me.

Alyssa flaps a sheet of paper in the air. "Finally. Here's the info sheet. Now I just have to find a pen for you." She digs in the box. "Pay dirt." She hands me a pen.

I fill in my name, phone number, and email.

She skims it, then drops the paper into a file folder. "A group of us run in the mornings. We're not super hard-core or anything, but we go for about three miles."

"I'm up for it."

She smiles. Her bottom teeth are a little crooked. "We finish at the Jitter Bean."

"I know where that is." We drove past it on our way in last night. It's only a few blocks from our house.

"Seriously addictive doughnuts. They have fruit and healthy food, too. Plus they sponsor us, so we try to show our faces there." With the edge of her hand, she smoothes a photocopied map. "Most runners hook up with us when we pass their house." She draws a misshapen circle, then adds arrows, a star with *start* above it, and a box with *The Jitter Bean* beside it. "Here's our route. Let's figure out what time we'll be at your place."

I check out the map, then point to my house. "This is where I live."

Her pen hovers over my street.

"Thirty-three Madison Road," I say. "The house with pink shutters."

I know I'm not imagining it when I see her hand shake as she marks an X.

CHAPTER 3

I walk home. From the end of the street I can see my mom pulling boxes from our truck. And I can hear Levi, my German shepherd, barking at something. We got in too late last night to unpack and only carried in the bare necessities to get us through until today.

"Levi," I call from the bottom of the driveway.

She bombs across the yard.

"What's in your mouth, girl?" She drops part of a peanut butter and jelly sandwich on the ground. Eww.

"How was school?" my mom asks.

"Fine." I scoop up the partial sandwich and toss it into the plastic trash bag in the truck. "I signed up for the team."

She shoots me a smile. "Help me with this box, will ya?"

I take one end, and we carry it up the sidewalk, stepping over the ugly, jagged crack that runs down the middle of the concrete steps leading to the porch.

"I think I'm going to like my new job," Mom says. "I had a good first day." She found a job and rented this house before we left Detroit.

I back through the door, bumping it open a little wider with my hip.

"Everyone in the office is friendly. They already invited me to Bunco."

That would be new and different. My mom making friends instead of attracting the closest loser.

We drop off the box in the kitchen, then head back outside.

My mom stops in the middle of the yard and points. "I'm seeing pansies here and here, maybe marigolds by the driveway, a hanging plant on the porch." She's into gardening but sticks to flowers that only last one season. They match our gypsy lifestyle.

She turns in a circle. "Don't tell me you can't see all the potential. This is the perfect place for a fresh start."

The narrow two-story house lists slightly to the left, as if it's trying to balance on one foot. The dried-out lawn is more weeds and dirt than anything else. The driveway gapes with potholes.

"I don't know, Mom," I say. "It's pretty ghetto." Seeing potential in everyone and everything is what gets her into trouble with guys.

There is one feature that jumps out and practically knocks you between the eyes. The shutters. The windows have pink shutters. Like someone was painting with cotton candy.

The house isn't big: two small bedrooms and a bathroom upstairs; a living room, kitchen, and half bathroom on the main floor. I open the door to the basement and peek from the top of the stairs. Unfinished, concrete floor, damp, creepy. Probably home to thousands of spiders. Ugh.

We finish hauling our stuff in from the truck. When we were packing, I marked the tops of boxes with a Sharpie, so it isn't rocket science figuring out where to pile them. I'm kind of a pro at moving.

"Let's tackle the beds," Mom says after I deliver the last BEDROOM: RAINE box.

It takes some maneuvering to get the frames and mattresses up the porch steps, through the door, and up the steep staircase. But it feels good to see the beginning of some sort of order. I'm not looking for potential, just to be settled.

"I'm hungry." Mom slaps her hands on her thighs once we've put the beds together. With her hair pulled back in a high ponytail and dressed in faded jeans and a Neil Young T-shirt, she could pass for my older sister. "I'll take the empty boxes to the basement if you start dinner."

"Deal." She knows my fear of spiders. When I moved in with my mother after my grandmother's death, I got bitten on the cheek by a spider. My face swelled up like a tangerine.

In the kitchen, I lift the flaps of a box labeled KITCHEN: DINNER, and nuke a couple of individual mac and cheeses while Mom opens a can of peaches and sticks in a spoon. It's our typical orange, first-dinner-in-a-new-place meal. Our fresh start begins with bright, processed food.

While waiting for the mac and cheese to cool, I feed Levi.

My mom scrounges in the box for her wine. She unscrews the lid, then splashes some into a mug. "You okay if I hit the sack early?"

I look at her puffy eyes and wan skin. "Sure." With just two of us, we have to watch out for each other. Although sometimes it feels like I'm doing more than my fair share of watching out.

"I'm going running with some of the girls at my school tomorrow morning," I say.

"That's great. Must be a good team if they're practicing in the summer." She waves a hand around the kitchen. "You pick up any memories in the house?"

"Not really." I stab pasta with my fork.

"Maybe there's not much for you to work with," she says. "With the house being vacant for close to two months."

I nod, chewing. She's probably right. Not that I have anyone to ask. My grandmother was the only other person I know who picked up memories, and she died when I was six. "I did get a man with a big gut yelling about kids and chores. It was on the doorknob to the hall closet."

"You could find that almost anywhere." My mom half smiles.

We pretty much finish our meal in silence. After yesterday's nine-hour drive from Michigan to New York, we're talked out. Yes, I said nine hours. Yes, my mother's a speed demon.

My mom fishes a sleeping pill from her purse and washes it down with the dregs of her wine. Then she sets her mug in the sink, stuffs her trash under the sink, gives me a hug good night, and clomps to the stairs.

Suddenly there's silence; she stopped partway up.

I poke my head around the corner and catch her pushing buttons on her phone. "You're not calling him, right?"

"I guess not." She shoves her phone in her pocket. The clomping resumes.

I'll be glad when she's over this recent loser. My favorite time is the break between boyfriends. With luck, Yielding will bring a long break.

The bathroom door thuds shut, and there's a whine as she switches on her electric toothbrush. My mom never skips brushing her teeth. It's one of the few things she sticks to in life. She's thirty-four years old and has never had a cavity.

I migrate into the living room and zone out with my computer, watching a movie I've seen a million times.

Eventually, Levi nudges me, pushing her head into my palm. "You interested in a walk, girl?" I ask.

The words are barely out of my mouth and she's racing to the door.

"Your choice," I say at the bottom of the driveway. "Which way?"

She sniffs the air like she's truly making a decision, then veers left.

I give a small nod to the skinny moon hanging low in the inky sky, as if to say, "Hi, it's us again. Same dog, same girl, different town."

A few cars rumble past. We set off a couple of motion-sensor lights. The odd night animal scurries away from us. It's an uneventful walk.

At the top of a tall hill, I plop down and hug my knees. It smells like summer, and the nighttime insects are noisy. Levi sits next to me, her flank pressing into my shoulder.

I gaze at the lights and the roofs that unfold like a paper fan, the possibilities stretching out. A little bubble of optimism bounces around in my chest at what's ahead. A chance to make friends, a chance to fit in, a chance to settle down long enough to go to Yielding High.

Detroit, more than five hundred miles away, is already blurring, like the icons on a computer that's shutting down. We lived there for the spring semester of seventh grade and most of this summer. I doubt anyone will even remember me.

I yawn and stand. "Let's go home."

The moon hides behind a cloud, making it darker as we tramp back. I'm not worried. It doesn't matter how many times we move; Levi always finds the way home.

She stops to pee next to a streetlight. Tacked to the pole is a missing-person flyer: Emily Huvar. She disappeared from Yielding a couple of months ago. The black-and-white head shot shows a girl with wavy, chin-length hair and large eyes. She's listed as thirteen years old. My age. I shiver even though it's still warm.

CHAPTER 4

*T*he next morning, I'm sitting on the sidewalk tying up my running shoes when I spot a group of heads bobbing toward me from down the street.

My lace breaks. Great. These shoes are trash. Maybe after a couple of paychecks, my mom can afford new ones for me.

I'm still knotting the lace ends together when the group jogs up.

Alyssa makes quick introductions. "Torie, Sydney, Willow, meet Raine."

Willow, a bobby pin in her mouth, ducks her head in hello.

Both Torie and Sydney have short hair, but Torie has

thick, ribbony blue streaks. Their eyes are wide open, as in wide open like they're at a horror show.

I go to say hi, when Torie blurts out, "How do you even handle living here?"

"What?" I fumble my shoelaces.

"In the dead girl's house."

"What?" I say.

"She's not necessarily dead," Willow says.

"Right. And I'm placing first in the West Hills Invite," Torie says, rolling her eyes.

"They're talking about Emily Huvar," Sydney explains.

Emily Huvar? That's the missing girl from the flyer. She lived in my house? Or I live in her house? She's dead? Goose bumps pop up on my arms.

"You about ready?" Alyssa says to me. "It's not like we have unlimited time."

"Yeah, sure." I quickly finish the knot and stumble to my feet.

"Talking pace, everyone," Alyssa says.

We take off, with Alyssa and Sydney ahead of me and Torie and Willow behind. I'm sandwiched in the middle, alone, trying to get my breathing and stride right. Trying to ignore the tingling in my fingers that's telling me there are sparkles around. Trying to shake the creeped-out feeling of sharing space with a missing-possibly-dead girl.

"Be glad Jennifer isn't working out today," Sydney says over her shoulder, as we cross a deserted park. "She always sets the pace too fast."

"She really keeps us moving," Willow adds, pushing an empty swing.

I bet I could keep up with whatever pace Jennifer sets. Or get a cramp trying.

"What's it like living in that house?" Torie bypasses the usual questions about where I came from and when I arrived. "How do you sleep at night?"

"I didn't know Emily Huvar lived there until you just told me," I say.

"The real estate people should've told you," she continues.

"They might've told Raine's parents," Sydney says, "and her parents didn't tell her because they didn't want to freak her out."

Torie nods.

So not plausible. My mom's big into over-sharing, all the way to Too Much Info and a little beyond. She hasn't heard about the Huvars. But she will, with her job as a property manager. Then she'll pass what she learns on to me.

"Emily vanished about two months ago, but her body still hasn't shown up," Torie says. "Even though the cops did a full investigation."

"At first there were lots of leads," Sydney says.

"People were calling in from all over, claiming they spotted her," Torie says. "In a Laundromat in Orlando. At a gas station in Idaho. Somewhere in Boston."

"But none of the tips panned out," Willow says. Wisps of hair flutter at the back of her neck where a couple of bobby pins are losing their grip.

We stop at a corner, standing still to conserve energy, waiting for a few other girls to join us. Alyssa's next to me but doesn't say a word, doesn't even make eye contact. Maybe she's in her zone. Or maybe she's just rude.

My fingers are going crazy. They're so itchy with tingles that I want to scrape them on the pavement. There must be a big sparkle on one of the girls.

We hit the road again.

"Raine lives in Emily Huvar's old house," Torie tells the girl running beside me.

"I personally think there's a chance she's alive," the girl says. "To me, no body means there's hope."

"She's dead," Torie says with ghoulish confidence. "Dead. Dead. Dead."

"Probably picked up by a pervert." The girl straightens her shoulders like she's got some authority on the subject. "My mom said that's why Yielding suddenly got a curfew for if you're under eighteen."

"I'm still not allowed to run alone," Willow says. "That's how nervous my parents are. They're worried the guy who got Emily will be back for more girls."

"I hope the police start investigating big-time again," Sydney says. "We shouldn't write her off. It's too soon to give up."

Torie shakes her head. "I bet there's nothing for the police to find here. A guy probably dragged Emily into his car, drove her somewhere, killed her, and dumped the body."

"There are stories of missing people who show up years later," Willow says. "Maybe Emily will return to Yielding in twenty years."

"The other day, there was a woman outside the grocery store with a petition to get the police to ramp the investigation back up," Sydney says. "She had pages of signatures."

Alyssa misses a step.

Willow grabs for her arm.

As Alyssa falls past me, her ponytail swings wildly, and I see the sparkle that's been driving my fingers nuts. It's winking at me from the underside of her hair clip.

Before thinking it through, before checking that nobody's watching, I seize the sparkle, trapping it in my fist.

Alyssa shakes Willow off her. "I'm fine, Willow. I just tripped," she says, her face one big look of irritation.

"You don't look fine," Willow says.

It's true. Alyssa's so pale, her skin matches the whites of her eyes. She bends over, massaging her ankle. "Keep going, guys." She waves impatiently with her free hand. "I'll catch up."

I glance around. Everyone's staring at Alyssa. Nobody's moving, not sure they should ditch her despite what she says. I close my eyes.

Alyssa and a slightly pudgy girl with short brown hair and a turned-up nose are standing in front of a display of eye shadow. Christmas music's playing in the background.

Alyssa unlatches one of the boxes. "Whew. Incredible amount of shades."

27

The brown-haired girl touches the palette with her baby finger. "They're so shimmery." She sucks in a breath. "And see how this entire row's flecked with gold."

Alyssa flips over the box and gasps at the price. "That's crazy expensive, Danielle."

"It's their limited edition," Danielle explains. "With their own unique pigments." She sounds like a commercial.

"What's this?" Frowning, Alyssa's nail hovers over a clear, colorless shadow.

"Smudge-proof base."

"I could definitely use that." Alyssa nods slowly, then looks at Danielle. "You can afford this?"

"Yeah. My mom's been paying me for all my good grades."

Alyssa rolls her eyes. "You're not even doing the work."

"I have to copy it over so it's in my own handwriting." Danielle tightens her grip around the box. "Besides, you're not doing your work, either."

"But I'm not getting any money for grades or for chores or for anything," Alyssa says. "My parents'll never pay me for grades. My stepdad's a jerk."

"Come on. We can go to my house and experiment with the different colors." Danielle carries the box to the front of the store.

I open my eyes to Alyssa and Willow staring at me. The others have gone ahead. I can't help but notice Alyssa's bare eyelids.

"You okay?" A worry line creases Willow's forehead.

"I'm fine. Just, uh, a little dehydrated," I say.

Alyssa shoos us with her hands. "Go, you guys. I'll catch up."

As Willow and I jog, she keeps glancing back to where Alyssa's putting weight on her foot and walking around.

I replay the memory in my mind. Danielle was one of the girls with Jennifer in the photo line. Alyssa and Danielle looked pretty much the same in the memory as they do now. So I'm guessing this happened last Christmas. It sounds like they're not doing their own homework. I wonder who's doing it for them.

"Did you drink *any* water before we started?" Willow asks me.

"No," I say sheepishly, like I'm a big moron, which is better than being a freak.

"That's not smart." Willow shakes her head and a bobby pin slides down her neck, hanging on a few strands of hair.

I shrug, like, *Hey, I know better, but stuff happens.*

"Don't get too weirded out by what Torie says about your house," Willow says. "She's a drama junkie."

"Did you know Emily Huvar?" I ask.

"Not really. We were in language arts and social studies together."

"Was she on the team?" I ask.

With her index finger, Willow pushes the bobby pin back into place. "She didn't do sports."

"It must be tough for her family," I say. My mom would

be a wreck if I disappeared and everyone thought horrible things had happened to me. "And tough for her close friends."

"It was hard on her family," Willow says slowly. "But she really didn't have any close friends. She wasn't the type."

"What do you mean?" I think people might describe me the same way.

"She transferred to Yielding last fall. Maybe if she'd been here longer, she would've made friends." Willow chews on her lip, thinking. "No, I don't think so. Emily was kind of strange. A huge loner." She looks back to make sure Alyssa's still out of hearing range. "Alyssa's group bullied her." She pauses. "To be funny."

I'm so sure they were going for humor when they picked on her. Not. They were going for the jugular. Because that's how mean girls operate.

Willow shakes her head and makes a face, embarrassed at saying only negative things about a girl who might be dead. "Emily was super smart, though. She was taking a computer class at the high school."

"Let's pick up the pace," Alyssa says, jogging up.

When we reach the others, they're still discussing Emily.

"Sydney's got this wild idea that Emily's living in Canada under a fake name. Maybe she switched the letters—" Torie starts.

Alyssa scowls. "No more talking," she says to the group at large. "We're pouring it on for the last hundred yards."

We get to the Jitter Bean red-faced, sweaty, and breathing hard. Everyone jostles to get through the door.

Inside smells of coffee and doughnuts. I think half the town's crammed in here, either chatting loudly or checking their phones.

We form a line.

Carrying a metal tray, a bald man approaches from the hall behind the counter. "Great timing, girls. They're piping hot."

Amid cheers, he slides the tray into the glass case, then brushes off his hands on his white apron.

"What are they?" I ask, gesturing at the mutant miniature doughnuts. They're missing holes and dusted with brown powder.

"Cappuccino delights," Torie says. "They were invented here. I mean, right here." She stomps on the linoleum floor. "Yielding might be in the backwater, but we've got some cool stuff going on."

"The filling is amazing," Willow says to me. "Indescribable. You have to try one."

The runners ahead of me carry their orders over to the tables.

"What can I get for you?" the bald man asks me.

"A frozen hot chocolate and a couple of cappuccino delights." I make a split-second decision. "To go."

I wave goodbye to the girls. A few wave back. Most of them are too busy talking and eating to notice me. Alyssa's rubbing her ankle.

In the parking lot, I hang a left and jog back to a certain streetlight, a streetlight I stopped at last night with Levi.

This time, I read Emily Huvar's missing-person flyer carefully.

MISSING: EMILY HUVAR

Height: 5'2"   Weight: 120 lbs.
Hair: brown   Eyes: brown
Age: 13

Last seen June 21 at 8:30 p.m. in the vicinity of Maple Street and Birch Avenue. She was wearing jeans and a solid purple T-shirt and was carrying a backpack.

At the bottom of the paper, there's a police file number and contact information.

Sucking on my straw, I stare at the photo. At her messy hair and round, sad eyes.

I'm walking in this girl's footsteps, around the house, on the way to school, through the halls. I've already met students she knew. I'll probably have a teacher she had.

Emily Huvar. Who was socially awkward. Who was super smart. Who didn't have friends. Who was picked on by the popular girls.

What happened to you?

CHAPTER 5

*T*he first thing I do when I get home is scour the place for sparkles left by Emily and her family. I don't come up with much. Under the upstairs bathroom vanity, I catch one of a small woman, on her knees, filling a box with stuff like shampoo, toilet paper, and tampons. Mrs. Huvar packing up? In the living room, I find a memory of Emily lying on the carpet, earbuds in, flipping through a magazine. And there's the vision I got before, of the man with the big gut shouting about chores. I don't check in the basement. I don't want to meet any spiders.

I wish my grandmother were still alive. She was so good at finding memories.

After inhaling a bowl of Lucky Charms, I shower, then spend a few hours on my room. I think of Emily as I tape up posters of my favorite bands, Panic Station and Cat's Cradle. They cover up the tape marks left by her posters. Slowly but surely, I'm taking over her space, erasing her. Someone will do the same to me in our old apartment in Detroit. It's just the way it works. The difference is, I didn't disappear. Nothing bad happened to me.

Downstairs, Levi paws at the front door, then stares up at me with a look that says, "You owe me. You abandoned me this morning. Come and sit outside while I pee."

I get my butt comfortable on the top step of the porch, my favorite mug—a photo mug of me running—filled with cold milk beside me. The chip out of the rim got bigger with this last move. I'm unfolding the paper bag with the cappuccino delights I saved from this morning when the next-door neighbor's door opens.

An older woman advances down her driveway and across the sidewalk. A faded checked housedress billows behind her.

She stops at the foot of our driveway. "Your dog should be on a chain or a leash. It's the law."

Really? Levi's curled up like a comma in a patch of shade on the lawn. But, in the interest of keeping things cool, I call to her. "Come here, girl."

She immediately trots over.

"Sit," I command, and she obeys, sitting up tall and straight, trying to impress.

"Does it bite?" the woman asks.

"She," I say. "No. Never."

She stomps up the driveway and over to me. "Did your parents know you were out by yourself last night?"

Eww. We have a creepy, annoying, spying neighbor.

"Did they?" She wags a finger at me.

I visualize my mom, comatose after her sleeping pill. "Sure."

"Hmpf." The crepey skin on her neck jiggles. "They think it's safe? Letting you wander around alone in the dark?" She pauses dramatically. "You know what happened to the other girl? And it was still dusk when she disappeared?"

"I wasn't actually alone," I say. "I had my dog."

She ignores me. "You'd think those parents would know better now, wouldn't you? But oh no. The younger sister still rides her bike around here. Unsupervised."

There's a sister? I never picked up a memory of her. Not that I got many memories, period. She must've shared the bedroom with Emily. My room.

"I'm glad your family moved in," the woman says gruffly. "I don't like a vacant house. Things happen in vacant houses."

"Like what?"

"Shenanigans. Teenagers sneaking in and getting up to shenanigans."

I suddenly remember the PB&J sandwich Levi found in the yard. Maybe someone sneaking into our house dropped it. That's a disturbing thought.

"Your dog still isn't on a leash." The woman turns and flounces down the driveway.

"Go get her, Levi," I whisper. "Go bite her right in her big checked butt."

Levi gazes at me solemnly, sitting as still as a statue. It's not hard to figure out which of us is better behaved.

I stretch out my legs and finish my cappuccino delights, which really rock as much as everyone says.

I'm increasingly curious about Emily Huvar.

"In you go, Levi." I nudge her through the front door, then get my laptop and head to the Jitter Bean for free Wi-Fi and air-conditioning.

The gold bell hanging from the doorknob tinkles when I walk in. A guy's restocking the stir sticks on the cart at the end of the counter. He looks up at the sound of the bell. It's the cute Frisbee guy. The guy who was making his friend laugh during school pictures.

He works at the Jitter Bean? But how? He's only in middle school.

The coffee shop is dead. Big difference from this morning. It still smells great, though. A Seattle Ska song is playing in the background.

I ask for a cup of water and go to the cart for a straw. Whistling along to the music, the guy has finished with the stir sticks and is working on loading up the napkin dispensers. A sparkle twinkles at me from his belt.

"You're new, right?" he says. "I saw you in the picture line at school."

My heart skips a beat. He noticed me? "Yeah. Just moved here."

"Sorry for slowing things down yesterday. Garrett and I have this ongoing competition to see who can make the other guy laugh so hard, he has his eyes closed for his picture."

"And?"

"Hopefully I pulled it off again. I don't want to break my three-year winning streak." He smiles, and his very blue eyes crinkle at the corners. "Can you believe they broke up after only one CD?" He nods at the Oily Artichokes logo on my T-shirt.

"I was so bummed." I tap the straw on the counter so that it busts through the paper.

"At least Seattle Ska are still going strong." He whistles a little more.

"Seattle Ska?" I make a face. "They're not even in the same league."

He looks at me like I just escaped from an insane asylum. And might be dangerous. "What's wrong with Seattle Ska?"

"Their lyrics. Can you say *incredibly lame*?" I make my fist into a microphone. " 'You have a hamster. My rug has dust mites. Your ex called again last night.' "

"That's probably not their strongest song," he says. "I'll give you that."

The bell on the door tinkles again.

In walks a super thin girl with short shorts and a tank top that looks like it spent a couple of hours on high in the dryer. She was in the picture room yesterday, laughing loudly.

She stands hips-touching close to the guy. "You didn't call me." She sticks out her lower lip.

"I'm at work. And you know how my dad is."

So that's how he's working here. It's a family business.

"Who's this?" She lifts a bony shoulder in my direction. Like I'm not a few inches from her and the owner of two perfectly functioning ears.

"I don't know," he says slowly, realizing he never asked my name. He grins. "Someone who doesn't like Seattle Ska."

"That's ridiculous," the girl says. "Everyone likes Seattle Ska."

"Well, apparently not everyone," I say.

She links an arm through his.

Oh, puh-lease. Could you be more unsubtle? I get it. He's your boyfriend. Or else you want him to be. It's not like I'm flirting with the guy. I don't even know if he's my type.

He unlinks his arm. "I gotta finish the cart." He looks at me. "I'm Hugh. This is Avalon."

"Raine." I haul my laptop bag off my shoulder and onto a nearby table.

"If you want online, the password's 'donuts are us,'" he says, then spells it. "There's a quiet room around the corner." He opens a drawer and pulls out a bunch of artificial sweeteners.

"Yeah, you probably want to use the back room," Avalon says, sorting the packets into different bowls.

Seriously? Comments like that make me want to follow Hugh around, flaunting some major hip action, just to get on her nerves.

The door opens again, and a couple of moms with strollers wheel in wailing babies. Maybe I do want that back room after all.

I pick up my cup. Then, my bag knocking against my side, I walk around the corner to peace and quiet.

I choose a table and chair near an outlet because my computer holds a charge for all of three seconds. Getting comfortable, I kick off my flip-flops and stretch out my legs. The air conditioner thuds on.

I spend a few minutes on Facebook. It doesn't take long because I don't keep in touch with many people. Then I hop over to the Yielding Middle School website. Great. There's a button that says ENGLISH SUMMER READING. I click. At least I've already read one of the three books.

I search for *Emily Huvar* plus *Yielding* plus *New York*. And come up with a boatload of hits.

There are photos of the family, showing Emily, who never smiles; a younger sister; a harried-looking mother; and a big-bellied father. Mr. Huvar was the frustrated man from the hall-closet-doorknob memory. And Mrs. Huvar was the kneeling woman from under the bathroom sink.

I click on an online report with a hundred or so

comments that are seriously all over the place, from parents questioning why Emily was out alone in the evening to a breeder of guard dogs to a mother who believes in microchipping babies at birth.

The best comments, the ones that say the most about Emily, were written by students.

> I wish now id sat next to you at lunch when you were eating by yourself

> you have a nice smile

> can someone tell her parents she still has my copy of a tree grows in brooklyn? The schools making me pay if i don't turn it in

> she's weird

> you made fun of my weight. Maybe you didn't mean to hurt my feelings, but you did

> I liked the poem you wrote for English

Then I hop over to an article from the *Albany Herald.*

June 28

Yielding Teen Still Missing

Last Saturday, thirteen-year-old Emily Huvar did what many typical teen girls do on a weekend evening. She ate dinner with her family, then loaded up her backpack and left on her bike a little after eight-thirty to spend the night at a slumber party with girl-friends. Emily was dressed in jeans and a purple T-shirt.

What happened next isn't so typical. Emily never arrived at her destination. She disappeared somewhere between her house and her friend's house, six blocks away.

Approximately three blocks from her destination, Emily met a fellow Yielding Middle School student on Maple Street. They talked briefly. Then Emily turned west on Birch Avenue. This was the last sighting of the teen.

The three girls at the sleepover didn't contact any adults when Emily did not show up. There had been some doubt as to whether her parents would allow her to attend.

Taxi logs and bus records shed no light on the teen's whereabouts. There are no reports of strange cars in the area. There have been no recent abductions in Yielding or in nearby towns. The Huvar family has not received a ransom note. Nor was a goodbye note left by the teen. Mrs. Huvar says her daughter packed only paja-mas, a change of clothing, and toiletries. The bike has not been found.

Emily Huvar's disappearance has rocked the small community of Yielding to the core. The girl has seemingly vanished into thin air.

If you have any information, please contact the Yielding Police Department at 555-476-8823. According to chief of police Joseph Bulkowski, every minute counts in a missing-person case. Emily Huvar has now been gone for eight days.

I watch a few news clips. Both of Emily's parents have foreign accents, but her mother's is way stronger, to the point that I only understand every other word. It doesn't help that she's in tears for most of the interviews. Emily's younger sister, Tasha, looks shell-shocked.

All the stuff I read says the same thing: the longer Emily's missing, the more likely it is she's dead.

An article from a local paper, the *Yielding Bugle,* is the most depressing. There's actually a graph with a line going down, down, down, showing that, at this late date, the chances of Emily's still being alive are dismal. I'm more likely to get an A in math.

I stumble across a black-and-white photo of Emily that's not a head shot. She's a petite girl, standing on our porch, leaning against the post at the top of the steps. I click to zoom in on her face.

She's looking straight into the camera, pulling me in with her huge, round, luminous eyes. They're the kind of eyes that follow you, the way the Mona Lisa's supposedly do. Eyes that reach out and say, "Whatever sadness you've seen in the world, I've seen worse."

I sit there for a minute, in a staring contest with her. Emily wins, of course.

CHAPTER 6

*O*n Tuesday morning, I wake up early. Even though I've changed schools more times than I've had birthday parties, I'm always angsty on the first day. Plus, I didn't sleep great. It takes a while to get used to the night sounds at a new place, but this house is particularly creaky and groany. Around three o'clock, I jerked awake, thinking for a minute I'd actually heard the back door open and close. Creepy.

At seven-thirty, I hoist my backpack over my shoulder and call to my mom that I'm leaving.

"Have a great day!" comes her muffled voice from behind the bathroom door.

✴

I find my math class and slip into a seat in the back. Between the knots in my stomach and the tingling in my fingers, I find it hard to concentrate on what the teacher is saying.

Walking down the hall between classes is more of the same. I want to be like everyone else and ignore the glinting memories. But I can't. Reaching for sparkles is like breathing. It just kind of happens. Sparkles help me figure out people, help me figure out how to fit in.

I manage to grab a couple, careful that no one's paying attention. I don't get any memories off them, though. That's annoying.

At lunch I eat alone in the noisy cafeteria. Nearby, a few girls from cross-country are sitting together. They nod but don't motion for me to join them. A few rows in front of me, Hugh's at a table with a bunch of guys. The redheaded guy, the one Hugh has the ongoing photo competition with, tries to start a food fight. Avalon shows up and squeezes in next to Hugh, so close you couldn't slip a piece of paper between them.

"Hi, Raine." Shirlee slides onto the bench opposite me. A sheen of sweat shines on her forehead. "This place is such a zoo. It's taken me almost all of lunch to find you."

"Yeah, I'm surprised they don't have more than one lunch period." I pop a potato chip into my mouth.

She swings her lunch bag onto the table.

It's easily the largest lunch bag I've ever seen. Every

school has their own rules. But I doubt it's ever cool to bring a lunch bag with a zipper as long as my arm.

Shirlee unzips the bag and pulls out a rectangular plastic container, snaps it open and lifts out a sandwich thick with sprouts and deli meat. "I wasn't prepared for how invisible I'd be here."

"It's only the first day," I say, understanding what she means.

With her baby finger, Shirlee nudges runaway sprouts back between the slices of bread, then opens her mouth wide. "When's your birthday, Raine?" she asks after she finishes chewing.

"May thirtieth."

"Place? Time? Year?"

"I don't do horoscopes," I say, clicking into why she's asking.

"Put the newspaper horoscopes out of your mind," she says, waving her sandwich. "It's not like that at all. It's subtle, all in the interpretation. Personally, I pick and choose my reading from several sources. I'm good at horoscoping."

"Uh-huh." I'm still not convinced.

"You'd be surprised what talents people have."

I think of how crazy Shirlee'd go if she knew I can pull memories off objects. How under the table, my fingers are dancing on my thighs, wanting to grab the sparkle I see on her dress.

Halfway through her sandwich, Shirlee sets it down and

pulls another container from her lunch bag. She flips up the lid and spoons out a weird-looking grainy thing.

"What is that?" I ask.

"Quinoa and mint salad." She tips the container in my direction. "Want some?"

"Maybe another time." Like when the world runs out of real food. I look at Shirlee with her food containers and dense whole-wheat bread and strange salad. She's wearing a dress with elastic under her boobs and around her arms. It might take Shirlee longer than the average girl to fit in here.

She reaches back into her lunch bag, this time pulling out oatmeal-and-raisin cookies.

A buzzer signals the end of lunch.

"Tell me," Shirlee pleads before we separate in the hall. "I'll just keep bugging you otherwise."

I sigh and tell her.

I spend the afternoon finding classrooms, finding seats, listening to welcome-to-my-class-here-are-the-rules speeches, sensing sparkles, seeing sparkles, jamming my hands in my pockets so they don't reach for sparkles. New schools are exhausting.

My last two periods of the day, science and film, are at opposite ends of the building, which means I have a major hike. As a result, I arrive late to film and end up standing at the front of the room, looking for an empty seat. Awkward.

The room is packed. Film is probably the most popular course at Yielding Middle. Everyone's taking it: Shirlee,

Jennifer, Alyssa, Danielle, Hugh, Garrett, Avalon, Willow, Torie, Sydney, and some students I recognize from my other classes.

Shirlee motions to a desk a few over from hers.

"Seattle Ska," Hugh says as I walk past him. His hair is still messy. Does he ever comb it? Would he look as cute with neat hair?

"Oily Artichokes," I reply.

Avalon scowls.

I slide into my seat. My backpack thuds to the floor.

The teacher looks up from where he's talking to a girl at his desk.

A couple of seats to the right of me, Jennifer leans forward. She's wearing this amazing necklace with an oversize teardrop stone that has the hugest sparkle hanging from it. "Alyssa," she whispers loud enough for everyone in a three-desk radius to hear.

Alyssa shifts toward Jennifer. "Yeah?"

"I think Shirlee got dressed in the dark this morning and put on her mother's dress."

As if someone flicked a switch, Shirlee turns bright red.

"Is that what happened?" Alyssa whispers at the same volume. "I thought it was a Goodwill special."

Danielle giggles.

Shirlee closes her eyes.

The teacher stands and claps his hands. "People. May I have your attention? We have a lot to get through in the next fifty minutes."

"You could just do half and let us out early," Garrett suggests.

Several students laugh.

"I've been warned about you, Mr. Lyons." The teacher frowns at Garrett.

Garrett smiles like this is some kind of honor.

"For those of you who don't know, I'm Mr. Magee." The teacher looks around. "You, in the blue shirt."

"Me?" I ask.

"Yes; would you get the papers from the counter at the back and pass them out?"

There's a sparkle sitting right in the middle of the stack. Just plopped there, waiting for me to scoop it up. I close my fist around it and shut my eyes.

It's a quick memory of my film teacher kissing my English teacher. Apparently, there's old-people romance at Yielding Middle. Gross.

After film, I head to the locker room to get dressed for cross-country. A bunch of us are almost finished changing when Torie marches in from outside. "Hurry up, girls. Chop-chop."

"Who died and put you in charge?" Jennifer says. The sparkle swings from her necklace.

Torie frowns. "Coach sent me. He said to remind you all how bad we want to get to state again this year. And that it's not gonna happen sitting around in here."

Girls start filing out. Only Jennifer and Alyssa take

their sweet time, chatting and hanging up clothes in their lockers.

I'm minding my own business, pulling on my shorts and T-shirt.

"So, you're friends with Shirlee?" Jennifer asks me. "Why?"

The best strategy with mean girls is to keep the conversation short and have as little to do with them as possible. That's one rule that doesn't change from school to school. "Shirlee's okay," I say.

"Okay if you like losers." Jennifer unclasps her necklace and drops it over a hook in her locker. The sparkle glints off the metal walls, lighting up the space like the North Star.

Alyssa laughs.

I grab my water bottle. Pushing open the door to the outside, I see the team stretching on the grass. They're in a big circle, with Torie in the middle, leading the warm-up. A man wearing a Cougars tank and a stopwatch around his neck stands behind her. He beckons to me.

"Raine, right? I'm Coach Jackson. Glad to have you on the team."

He asks about my running experience, then does what every coach does and sticks me with his slow group. I know I can keep up with the fast runners, but I have to prove it. Again. This gets old.

Willow scoots over to make room for me in the warm-up circle.

Jennifer and Alyssa arrive. Without a word, Torie vacates her position, and Jennifer takes over leading the exercises.

The coach surveys us as we stretch, discusses today's speed interval training, and pulls out players for private chats about goals and skills. It's your typical beginning-of-the-season practice.

Eventually, he blows his whistle. "Let's get started on the track. We'll keep it easy today. Two hundreds at a no-talking pace."

I can handle this. In my sleep.

He pulls stopwatches from a gym bag and tosses one to Jennifer, who leads the fast group, including Alyssa, Torie, and Sydney, to the track.

Still working on my hamstrings, I watch their sets. Jennifer stays easily in the lead. She's a natural, one of those runners who drives coaches crazy. She lands on the ball of her foot and has a short arm swing, but she's quick. And because she's quick, she won't change what she's doing wrong.

I'm in Willow's group.

I run out in front. With each bouncy step on the cushioned track, I concentrate on getting a rhythm with my legs, my arms, my lungs. I'm reaching for that place where my mind is clear. Where all I do is run. I don't stress about being the new kid on the block. I don't stress about my mother falling for another deadbeat. I don't stress about moving again.

Willow and I end up running an extra two hundred together. I'm sure she's vying for a spot on the fast team, too. The coach's eyes are on us, and I keep my back straight and my stride long.

"Make your face blank," I say to her out of the side of my mouth. "So you don't look tired."

She gives a quick nod and adjusts her expression.

When we're done, I veer off the track to where my bottle of water lies in the grass.

"Good job, Raine," Coach calls out.

"Good job, Raine. We're so happy to have you on the team," Jennifer says sarcastically, then jogs past me.

Back in the locker room, Jennifer and Alyssa unpack towels and shampoo and set them on the bench. Then they walk to the drinking fountain around the corner.

Jennifer's locker door is open, and the necklace swings gently from the hook. Its sparkle shines at me, practically poking out my eyes with its sharp brightness. What kind of memory does it hold?

I take a step toward it. Could I grab the sparkle without anyone noticing? What if I pretend to trip and fall against the bank of lockers? Could I quickly reach in? There are a lot of girls around who might notice I have a hand in Jennifer's stuff.

I take another step. I would love to get something big on her. Something so embarrassing it would make her shut up and swallow her meanness if I shared it. Maybe that something is on the incredibly bright sparkle. The sparkle from her purse was about an older guy telling her to get lost. Could the memory on the necklace be even more personal than that?

Willow taps my shoulder, and I jump.

"Thanks for the tip, Raine." She smiles. "I really appreciate it."

"No big deal," I say.

Jennifer and Alyssa return from the drinking fountain and pick up their things from the bench.

"Wait. I need conditioner." Jennifer seizes a pink bottle from inside her locker. Then she slams the door and clicks on the lock, shutting away the necklace.

At least for now.

CHAPTER 7

$\mathcal{A}$fter about a week at Yielding Middle, I'm already in a groove. Go to school. Go to practice. Do homework. Eat dinner. Walk the dog. Do more homework.

I slam my math textbook shut. "Come on, Levi. My brain needs a break."

Outside, I swat the first mosquito of the evening off my forearm. As we walk, words like *variable, coefficient,* and *factor* swarm in my head. Yielding's ahead of my Detroit school in math. There's no way I'll be ready for tomorrow's quiz.

I'm so lost in the world of math misery that I only vaguely hear someone calling, "Buttons. Buttons!" before I finally look up to see Hugh.

The second I spot him, everything polynomial flees from my mind, and I smile. A dog the size of a toaster is dragging Hugh along the sidewalk.

Levi and I stop to watch the show.

"Buttons, slow down!" At the end of a taut leash, Hugh's zigzagging all over the sidewalk.

Buttons stops short when he spots Levi.

"How do you get your dog to just sit there?" Hugh asks. "She's not even on a leash."

"It's all about who's boss in the relationship."

"Wow. Thanks," Hugh says, looking fake hurt.

"I may have had a little help from a place called Doggy Discipline," I admit.

We begin walking side by side, following Buttons's lead. I'm not always good at joking around with a guy, especially a cute guy. But maybe knowing about him and Avalon takes off all the pressure, and I'm pretty at ease. There's a sparkle on his back pocket. I don't make any attempt to grab it. I'm curious to see what I think of Hugh without reading one of his memories. I want to see how we get along the normal way.

At the corner of Maple and Birch, Hugh puts on the brakes, his footsteps turning slow and heavy like he has bricks for feet. For the first time, Buttons isn't straining at the leash.

"You know about Emily Huvar?" Hugh asks.

"Yeah," I say. "I live in her old house."

"I didn't realize that." He looks surprised. "I saw her

that last night." He points to the sidewalk. "Right about here."

So Hugh was the student who saw Emily on her way to the sleepover.

"I was out being dragged by Buttons, and suddenly Emily was off her bike and wheeling it next to me, talking a mile a minute about the sleepover and the other girls and a science project and the pizza they were ordering. Then she petted Buttons and started telling me the tricks her dog could do and that Buttons would be lucky if he learned to sit."

"That's harsh," I say.

"Yeah." He shrugs. "I didn't mention that Buttons got his name because of eating a buttload of buttons. And that we basically can't train him to do anything. He's years away from sitting on command."

I laugh. "I don't think I would've mentioned that, either."

We start walking again.

"It's kind of weird living in the same house," I say. "Is it weird being the last person who saw her?"

He nods. "People asked me a lot of crazy questions when it first happened." With his free hand, he pushes his hair off his forehead. It immediately flops back. "But mostly, I just feel bad because normally I walk the way Emily headed when she turned on Birch. That's the route I always take, always. But I wanted to get away from her, so I kept going straight on Maple.

"If I'd walked her to Jennifer's house, I could've made a difference."

"Jennifer's house?"

"Yeah. Jennifer Swearingon."

"Is that the same Jennifer who hangs out with Alyssa and Danielle?" I ask incredulously.

Hugh nods like this is nothing strange.

Seriously, guys are so clueless when it comes to social stuff. The Emilys of middle school do not get invited to sleepovers by the Jennifers. That's like saying I'll wake up fluent in Spanish. Or my mother will marry a stable guy with a full-time job and a bank account and live happily ever after in the same house until she dies. Willow even said Alyssa and her friends picked on Emily.

"Where's Jennifer's house?" I ask.

"It's the last two-story on Birch."

Maybe Jennifer's mom forced her to include Emily? Or maybe the girls never planned to answer the door when Emily arrived. Or maybe they were going to make her play a humiliating game of Truth or Dare. I don't get it. It's all too weird.

We walk a couple more blocks together.

"I live up this way." Hugh inclines his head toward a cul-de-sac. "See you at school."

Buttons's yips fade as he and Hugh get farther away.

What if I found a memory of Emily's from that night? Levi and I double back to Birch. I hold out my arms, tuning into my fingers and any sparkles they might sense, and think Emily thoughts.

Levi slows to my pace, occasionally bumping against my knee.

My fingers begin to tingle at a house that's lit up both inside and out. There's a large living room window with a couple sitting on a couch watching TV.

I squint, looking for a sparkle. Nothing. "Levi, stay here," I whisper, pointing to the sidewalk.

She whines, not wanting me to leave her.

"Shhh." I put a finger to my lips. Then I creep up the side of the driveway, staying as close to the hedge as possible. The tingling in my fingers gets stronger. My palms go sweaty. Where is a sparkle? I blink and open my eyes wide.

There it is. Glinting weakly, a small sparkle hangs from the garage door handle. I dash from the hedge to the middle of the garage, crouching down and flattening myself against the door. I reach out to trap the sparkle.

A motion light blasts on.

I stifle a scream.

The front door doesn't open. No one appears at the living room window. I tell my thudding heart to cut it out. The motion light's probably activated a million times each night by small animals and cars.

I close my eyes to see the memory.

It's a man talking with another man about weed killer. Earth-shattering. Not.

Birch is a long street, and I actually find several memories on it. There's a woman who dashes out in pajamas to steal her neighbor's newspaper. A man who doesn't pick up after his dog. A group of high school kids toilet-papering a house. A couple making out. But I don't find anything to do with Emily.

"This is stupid," I say. "We should go home."

Levi looks at me, waiting for a definite decision.

"Whatever. We're this close. We might as well see what Jennifer's house looks like."

Near the end of the street, we stop at the last two-story house.

It's magazine cute, with a green lawn surrounded by a little fence. The beds under the windows are full of flowers. Lights line the stone walkway leading to the front door. The place looks like a home for a perfect, happy family where generations of relatives come to celebrate Thanksgiving and everyone gets along. Hard to believe that something horrible happened to Emily on the way to this house.

I take a few steps onto the driveway and stretch out my arms. Immediately, my fingers begin to tingle. My heart tries to hammer its way out of my chest. I don't want to be busted on Jennifer's front yard. What would I say? "Hi, I was out walking my dog and got lost in front of your house"?

Sparkles are often easier to spot at night, but I'm seeing nothing here. I'm about to give up when my eye catches a twinkle. It's a small, dullish sparkle, barely bright enough to have a shadow, on the short wooden fence.

I hope it's not a memory of another couple making out. Two steps take me to the fence. Levi follows, sniffing at the bottom of a post. I reach out.

There's a grinding sound. The garage door's opening.

I stop breathing. My heart stops beating. My blood probably stops flowing through my veins.

A sleek black car backs out.

"Levi," I whisper. "Lie down."

I flatten myself into the fence, pressing up tight against the hard wood, repeating over and over in my head, "Please don't see me. Please don't see me. Please don't see me."

The car reverses slowly, then stops.

The driver's window rolls down. "I hope you have a plastic bag with you," a woman says. She's an older, plumper version of Jennifer. Must be her mother.

I pull the grocery bag from my pocket and wave it.

"Good," she says. "We've been having a problem with someone not taking care of their dog's business." The window rolls up, and the car roars down the street.

I begin breathing. My heart begins beating. I place my hand on the fence, over the sparkle.

It's Emily's memory.

CHAPTER 8

It's dusk. Emily stands in front of Jennifer's house, leaning against the fence. Tucked under her arm is a shoe box. She breathes, and a puff of air escapes from her mouth. She contemplates the house, then glances at the mailbox at the end of the driveway.

A breeze blows Emily's hair across her face. When she pushes it away, she accidentally loosens her hold on the shoe box, and it drops to the ground. She quickly picks it up, pulls off the lid, and checks inside. A plastic figure of a Native American has fallen over, and she stands it up in the corner. Her gloved fingertips brush against plastic wolves, making sure they're stable. She straightens a miniature dogsled.

A light flicks on in the living room. Jennifer crosses the room, backlit. She goes to the window and lowers the blinds. Emily steps toward the front door.

In the distance, a car honks. Is Jennifer's mom returning?

"Levi," I say. "Let's go."

We run home—fast, as if wild wolves are chasing us. The memory's not from the night Emily disappeared. She wasn't dressed in a purple T-shirt, and she wasn't carrying a backpack. She had on a winter jacket, gloves, and boots. This memory is from a different night, a cold night. Still very creepy.

Breathing heavily, I run past our truck, then take the steps to the porch two at a time. I pull open the door and am hit by the smell of frying onions and garlic. I go into the kitchen and straight to the cupboard with the glasses.

"You okay?" my mom asks. She's at the stove, deep in stir-fry mode.

"Yeah," I say, gulping water. "Fast run."

"I hope you're hungry." She smiles. "I went overboard." She scoops food from the wok onto two plates and carries them to the bar.

I pour a glass of water for my mom and refill mine. I'm ravenous, but I don't think I can eat. I feel like I'm plugged into a wall socket and current is humming through me. "You know anything about the people who lived here before us?"

"A little. The Huvars. They were the topic of conversation today at lunch." She dumps soy sauce over her meal.

Eating Chinese is really just an excuse for my mom to drink soy sauce. "Mr. Huvar applied for a job as handyman for one of our complexes."

"Will he get it?" My mind flits back to Jennifer's house. What was Emily doing there? What's the connection between the meanest girl in school and the girl who disappeared?

My mom shrugs. "It's not up to me, but I hope so. That family has had a run of really bad luck. The dad lost his job, and they couldn't keep up with the rent. They were in the process of being evicted from this house when their daughter disappeared. She's never been found. She was your age."

Standing by the fence with her shoe box, Emily wasn't freaked out. It was more like she was making a decision. She seemed like she was at Jennifer's for a reason, like she had a right to be there.

"Earth to Raine. Aren't you eating?"

"What? Oh, sure." I spear the smallest piece of pineapple and the smallest piece of chicken with my fork.

"And you never did pick up any of the girl's memories in the house?" She dunks a chunk of chicken in a puddle of soy sauce.

Emily decided not to leave the shoe box in the mailbox, especially once she saw Jennifer was home. Could I have looked more closely at the shoe box Emily was holding? I've never tried that with a memory, zeroing in on part of it.

"What?" I tune in to my mom. "Memories in the house? I saw her reading a magazine in the living room."

"Really?" My mom stops eating. "What did she seem like?"

"I don't know," I say. "Like a girl lying on the carpet with earbuds in and flipping pages."

Right here is the moment when a different daughter with a different mother might give up more details. But I'm not into sharing. I've been so independent for so long, I'm used to working through things for myself. Sometimes, like now, I feel like I'm going to explode. But that's just the way I do it. And because my mom never got into the mother role, she doesn't think to quiz me to death. I mean, we were basically apart for the first six years of my life. She was away, making mistakes, growing up, trying new things, only showing up to see me for some of the holidays. I'm not sure she would've returned when she did except that my grandmother died, and someone had to take care of me. Also, my mother can't read memories. It's another thing that separates us.

After dinner, she watches reality TV while I kind of do homework. My mind is more on Emily than on the periodic table or ancient Rome. Emily's a splinter in my brain.

At ten, my mom flips over to the news.

The lead story is a fire that burned forty acres of nearby forest. The fire chief is treating it as arson because there was some sort of timer at the scene.

"Not another fire," my mom says, trundling into the

kitchen during a commercial. She returns with her wine and sleeping pills.

"I'm having a lot of trouble sleeping here," I say.

"This house was built in the late forties." She pops off the lid of her pill vial. "It has more old-age creaks than most places we've lived."

A little later, I close my books and drop them in my backpack. "Are you up for a walk, Levi?"

Like I had to ask? She's panting at the door before I even have one shoe on. We head back to Jennifer's and to the memory on the fence.

When I get to the part where Emily's fixing what fell over in the box, I slow down my breathing, moving through the memory at snail speed. I zoom in on every detail, from the cold air escaping Emily's mouth to the tight weave of her gloves. I catch a glimpse of a typed label on the lid. Rewind. FA. Rewind again. FANG. Rewind again. FANG is the most I can see of the first line. Emily's thumb covers the word next to it.

Emily's hand shifts as she goes to fit the lid back on. I see the second line clearly: BY JENNIFER SWEARINGON.

I open my eyes. Wham. Everything drops into place. Like when you're doing a jigsaw puzzle, and suddenly you're on a roll and can piece together a whole section in two seconds flat.

FANG. As in *White Fang.* I guess it's a pretty famous book, because we read it for seventh-grade language arts in Detroit, too. Emily was delivering a diorama based on *White*

Fang to Jennifer. She was doing Jennifer's homework, or at least some of it. Was Emily also doing Alyssa and Danielle's homework? Willow said Emily was super smart.

Now I get why Emily was invited to a sleepover at Jennifer's.

Homework payment.

CHAPTER 9

*O*n Monday morning, I'm surprised to see Shirlee and her lunch bag sitting on the curb at the bottom of my drive-way. It's not like we walk to school together.

"Hi, Raine." She opens her arms dramatically. "I put together a reading for you."

My eyes roll of their own accord. I can't help it.

Shirlee doesn't seem to notice. "Someone has a crush on you."

Hugh actually springs into my mind, his hair as unkempt as ever. I push him out. Guys with girlfriends are not okay.

I start toward school, and Shirlee hurries to catch up.

"How about I win the lottery instead?" I say. "I could use the money."

"You'll have your best report card ever this semester," she says, ignoring my comment. "And you'll come in first for two running events this year."

"Wow," I say, while we wait at an intersection for a break in traffic. "Welcome to my incredible life."

"I have to admit, I'm kinda jealous," Shirlee says. "I checked your reading five different ways, which is, yes, excessive. But I wanted to be sure."

If, and that's a huge if, I believed in any of this craziness, I'd tell Shirlee to run my mom's horoscope. That would be the best way to predict what's around the corner for me.

Before sixth period, I duck into a bathroom. The second I push open the door, I know something bad is happening.

Danielle has her arms folded across her chest. "Maybe you want to use a different bathroom." She looks tough, but her voice comes out reedy and nervous.

"Why?" I look past her.

The doors to both cubicles are closed. There's a line of six girls. Shirlee's the first one. Jennifer's by her side.

Shirlee turns to look at me. Her eyes are glassy with tears.

What's going on?

A cubicle door swings open, and Shirlee steps forward.

"I don't think so." Jennifer quickly elbows in front of her. "You're next," Jennifer says with a dazzling smile to the girl who's second in line.

A few seconds later, a toilet flushes and the other cubicle

door opens. Alyssa exits, holds the door wide open, blocking Shirlee, and ushers in another girl from the line.

Each time Shirlee makes an attempt to get to a cubicle or to leave the bathroom, either Jennifer or Alyssa heads her off.

The girls in line are quiet, keeping their eyes on the floor. They take their turn, wash their hands, then blow out of there as fast as possible. They're not torturing Shirlee, but they're not helping her, either. No one wants to face the consequences of crossing the mean girls.

"No cutting," Alyssa orders when Shirlee tries to get past her.

"I'll go to another bathroom," Shirlee squeaks.

Alyssa shakes her head.

Shirlee crosses her feet.

How long has this been going on?

"We'll let you know when you can leave." Jennifer watches me as she says this, challenging me.

I've never turned down a challenge. In fact, I ended up with a broken arm over a challenge to jump off the monkey bars in fifth grade. You might say I'm challenge-challenged.

Jennifer and Alyssa go back to bullying Shirlee.

The girls in line shuffle forward. Large tears stream down Shirlee's cheeks. "I just want to go home," she hiccups.

"Come on, Jennifer," Danielle says. "That's enough."

Jennifer glares.

"So, Jennifer," I say, all perky and fake friendly, "what's

the deal with Michael?" I never know when or if someone's memory will come in handy. But right now seems like the perfect time to bring up the memory I pulled off Jennifer's purse on registration day.

Jennifer's whole body stiffens. Even her hair loses some of its cute bounce.

The restroom goes silent. Shirlee stops hiccupping.

"You know what he told me?" I lean toward her, like we're best buds. "That he had to kick you out of his car. He just wants you to get lost and leave him alone." I stick out my lower lip in a pout. "Sorry. I know that hurts."

Jennifer's face drains of color.

Shirlee slips into a cubicle, and there's a click as she locks the door.

Jennifer stares at me, her eyes feverish with hate. I stare right back. She'll make me pay for this.

The buzzer rings loudly in the hall.

Jennifer turns on her heel and flounces out. Alyssa follows, giving me a wide berth, like I might be very, very bad luck. Danielle nods, and the tiniest smile flits across her face.

The restroom empties fast. Well, except for Shirlee, who's still in the cubicle, peeing like she drank a twelve-pack of soda.

While she's washing her hands, Shirlee focuses on the running water. "Thanks," she says softly. "You saved my life."

"At least your bladder," I say.

"How'd you know about Jennifer and that guy?"

"Just heard it around."

In film, I sit next to Shirlee. Jennifer and I ignore each other.

We're still ignoring each other at practice. Jennifer's leading the exercises, and I'm following along, but it's like there's a wall of ice between us.

Coach pulls me out of the circle.

"Raine, you're looking good, real good." He taps his clipboard. "You're a natural runner, and you're paying your dues, doing what it takes to improve."

"Thanks," I say.

"Our first invite," he says, "gives the top three finishers gift certificates to At Full Speed in Albany. Not too shabby, eh? With your times, you can be in there."

A gift certificate for At Full Speed? I could get new running shoes.

"Jennifer," he calls, "I want you and Raine doing sprints together today."

Jennifer doesn't answer or even react. It's as if she's deaf.

I blow out a breath. Just what I didn't want.

After warm-ups, she walks briskly to the track. I'm right next to her.

We stand side by side, waiting to start. Jennifer's mouth is set in a straight line, and determination is flowing off her. She wants to beat me so bad, she's practically pawing the ground like a racehorse.

We take off, and she edges in front and stays there. I'm pounding the track, trying to get it together, trying to get the timing right with my arms, legs, and lungs. But it's like they're all operating separately, as if they belong to different bodies.

Jennifer's fueled by the Michael comments. For her, it's payback time on the track. She blows me out of the water on the second, third, and fourth sprints.

At some point, I notice Hugh. He and Avalon are walking hand in hand on the asphalt at the back of the school. She leans into him, and he puts his arm around her.

Jennifer whips my butt again. I look up and see Hugh watching. I flush. Why do I care if someone else's boyfriend sees me totally sucking?

The coach walks over to us, his whistle bumping his chest. He jerks his head at me, frowning. "Raine, get your head in the game."

Even this doesn't get a reaction from Jennifer. Eyes squinting, neck thrust forward, she's in her zone for the next sprint, getting ready to go for the kill again.

Finally, the frustrating and humiliating practice comes to an end. No one from the team speaks to me or even looks at me, and I walk alone across the grass to the locker room.

I'm almost at the door when Jennifer sidles up next to me. "You're pathetic."

CHAPTER 10

I jolt awake in the middle of the night, breathing hard, my stomach cramping. I dash to the bathroom and throw up.

Eventually, I crawl back between the sheets, turn off the alarm on my phone, and fall into the heavy sleep of the sick. I vaguely remember my mother trying to wake me up for school, then promising to call the absence line.

By the time I drag myself out of bed, the sun is a big yellow ball high in the sky. Levi's in my face with her doggy breath. And Mom's long gone to work. The house is as quiet as a morgue.

I stumble downstairs to the kitchen, prop myself up at the counter, and nibble on dry toast.

Out of the corner of my eye, I catch a turquoise blur.

With small steps, I make it to the window. It's a girl wearing a turquoise bike helmet. She's flattened against the tree in the backyard, a plastic grocery bag dangling by her side. Her head's turned toward the nosy neighbor's house. Suddenly, and I can practically see her counting *one-two-three* in her head, she dashes around the corner to the back of our house, where she's hidden from the neighbors and the street.

I cross the kitchen to the back door.

I'm at the stairs in time to hear a key clicking in the lock. The doorknob turns. The door swings open.

"Hello," I say.

She screams. The grocery bag she was carrying thuds to the floor. A couple of sandwiches wrapped in waxed paper and a banana roll out, followed by a copy of *Wired,* a magazine about computers and technology. The name on the address label says EMILY HUVAR.

The girl's gaze darts nervously around the kitchen.

I recognize her from pictures online. Tasha Huvar, Emily's little sister. She's a mini Emily, with the same big eyes and wavy hair. I'm guessing she's around ten. "You're Tasha Huvar, right?" I say.

She shrugs, and her helmet slides a little down her forehead.

Levi eyes the sandwiches.

Tasha quickly kneels to scoop everything into the bag.

How incredibly sad is this? She's carrying around a

magazine like it's her sister's stuffed animal. And ditching school to eat lunch in the house where they used to live. Normally, there'd be no one here at this time.

She stands.

"You need to give me the key." I hold out my hand. With my other hand, I grasp my stomach, which is gurgling again.

Tasha backs up a couple of little steps, staring at my outstretched hand, then at the key. Desperation crosses her face. Slowly, she passes it to me. It's sticky.

"You have any more copies?" I ask.

Her eyes on her sneakers, she looks so unhappy that I'm sure she really doesn't have an extra key at home.

"How often do you come here?" I wipe the sweat off my forehead. I must have a huge, raging fever. "You shouldn't be skipping school."

Her gaze stays on her sneakers, and her mouth stays shut.

"Tasha?"

Her face is as vacant as a blank sheet of paper. Even when I say her name.

And I finally get it. I get why she isn't answering my questions. I get why she thinks she's tricking me with her baby steps toward the back door. I get why she doesn't question how I know her name. Tasha isn't completely with it.

She must feel closer or something to her sister when she's here. "You want to eat in the kitchen today? One last time?" She has no idea what this offer is costing me. I just want to crawl back to bed. And die.

"No."

Levi slinks past me and rubs against Tasha's leg. Tasha scratches Levi behind the left ear, right at her favorite spot. It usually takes Levi ages to warm up to someone new. These two are obviously best friends. How many times has Tasha snuck in?

"I'm Raine. Looks like you already know Levi," I say.

She nods, opens the door, and steps out.

Levi and I follow her to the side of the house where her bike, also turquoise, is propped against the wall.

"Levi jeans." Tasha plops the bag in the wicker basket hanging from her handlebars.

"You're right. She's named after the jeans," I say. "When she was a puppy, she was really whimpery. She only calmed down when I held her. One night I put a pair of my jeans in her bed, and she went right to sleep."

Tasha smiles. "My dog was Pes."

"That's a cute name."

"It means 'dog.'"

"Yeah?" This strikes me as funny, but Tasha's eyes are wide and serious.

"Pes ran away," she says. "He has a new family."

Her family gets evicted. Her sister disappears. She loses her dog. Can you say *tragic*?

Tasha pushes up her helmet. There's a red line across

her forehead where it was pressing. She slides a foot in a pedal and swings her leg over the bicycle seat.

"Bye, Levi Jeans," she says. "Bye, Raine."

She rides across our bumpy lawn to the driveway, then onto the street. The afternoon sun bounces off her turquoise helmet. Red streamers flap and flutter from where they're wound around the handles. Her back rigid and her bony elbows jutting out, she pedals in a straight line.

CHAPTER 11

A bunch of kids are absent the next day. It's as if zombies infested our school and feasted on a large percentage of the student population. The stomach flu has hit Yielding Middle with a vengeance.

Mr. Magee is absent, too, and we have a sub in film. She's young and dressed in jeans, a colorful scarf tossed around her neck. Hunched over the teacher's desk, she's totally engrossed in a paperback, not even lifting her eyes while we file in.

Once we're somewhat settled, she lays her book facedown. "Your teacher left instructions for the next project, and you have all of today's class to work on it. Choose a partner, then pick up a handout." She stands long enough to plop a stack of papers on an empty desk by the door. Then she returns to her book.

"But half of us are missing," Jennifer complains, not bothering to raise her hand.

She has a point. Torie and Sydney are seated next to each other and will no doubt pair up. Shirlee's absent. Which leaves me with no one. Jennifer's in a similar boat. Both Alyssa and Danielle are absent, and I'm sure she doesn't want to lower herself to work with a loser like me.

"Just show us a video," Jennifer says.

The sub shrugs. "Your teacher didn't leave anything but this assignment." She waves her book in the air. "I'm doing my master's and have a test on this. Tonight."

In other words, she's here to babysit while getting her own homework done.

With a loud sigh, Jennifer sticks out her feet and leans back in her chair, her arms crossed over her chest.

A shadow falls across my desk. "Wanna work together?" Hugh asks.

My heart revs a little until I realize that Avalon is one of the missing. Garrett, too. I'm just the best of his few options. "Sure," I say.

"Great," he says. "Let me grab our handouts."

Jennifer flounces to the substitute. "I need a pass to see the nurse."

I swear the sub doesn't even break from reading to fill out the form. That's some incredible focus. I bet she aces her test.

There's a bang as Jennifer lets the door slam behind her.

"You ever heard of the Albany Boys?" Hugh asks, pushing a desk against mine.

"No."

"I think they're your kind of band. I'll send you a link to one of my playlists."

"Would there happen to be any Seattle Ska on that playlist?" I ask, raising my eyebrows.

He hesitates. "Definitely not."

"Liar."

Hugh smiles. "You can always skip the Seattle Ska tracks."

"I plan to."

He smiles again.

"Produce a ten-minute video pertaining to Yielding," I read from the handout.

We look over the guidelines and brainstorm for three seconds, then drift into joking around and chatting about school, gaming, and of course, music. It's like we can't stop talking.

When the volume level in the room gets a little high, the sub looks up from her book. "Put a lid on it, guys." Other than that, she ignores us.

"We didn't accomplish much," I say at the end of class. The page in my notebook only has a few ideas on it.

"We should probably get together later," Hugh says. He checks his phone. "How about Thursday of next week?" He grimaces. "Is that okay? If it's not till next week? I'm working a lot, and I'm in the gaming club, and we have an event."

"As long as we work independently before then." I put my notebook and pen in my backpack.

"If we meet at the Jitter Bean, my dad'll throw in free drinks and doughnuts."

"Not that you have to bribe me."

"Six-thirty?" Hugh stands. "That's probably the earliest I can be there."

"Sure." I open my arms wide enough to include Hugh, me, the two desks. "Avalon'll be okay with this?"

"Sure." He looks surprised. "Why wouldn't she be?"

I shrug. *Maybe because she acts like you two are Siamese twins.*

Surprisingly, Jennifer shows up for cross-country. I thought she'd use the nurse's pass to get out of practice. Maybe she's hoping to humiliate me at sprints again.

But today practice is good. I run well enough that Coach throws me a compliment. Jennifer frowns at this, making practice even better. I'm headed home now, humming, feeling like life doesn't suck. Just as I cross onto my street, someone calls my name.

It's Shirlee, slouched against the stop sign. She looks like death, her face blotchy and gray, her eyes red-rimmed.

"Shirlee?" I say. "Shouldn't you be home in bed?"

She sniffs loudly and slides down the post until she's sitting on the ground, hunched over like a snail shell. And then she starts crying.

I drop my backpack and sit next to her.

The sobbing slows, then trickles to a raggedy stop. She takes a few deep, shuddery breaths. "I want to quit school," she says to the ground between her knees.

"What?"

"I want to quit school."

Totally didn't see that coming. I scan her for a sparkle but don't see anything. And I'm not getting any tingling messages from my fingers. It would be so nice if a sparkle showed up when I needed one to make sense of a situation.

Shirlee starts sniffling, and her eyes fill with tears again.

"You could quit, right?" I say. "Go back to home-schooling?"

"My mom won't let me."

"Anything in your horoscope that would convince her?" I can't believe those words just came out of my mouth.

"She's not into astrology."

I don't answer, digesting this. Somehow I had the impression Shirlee came from an entire family of Shirlees.

"What's going on?" I ask when we're up and walking.

"It's Jennifer." She blinks rapidly. "She's horrible."

"I agree."

Suddenly I get this mental slide show: Shirlee in film, pale and quiet while Jennifer talks to her. Shirlee in the cafeteria, practically under the table, pretending to look for something when Jennifer walks by. And then, of course, Shirlee like a trapped animal in the restroom. The bullying's been escalating right in front of me, but I never noticed. I feel bad. "Stand up to her. That's the only way to stop her."

"I can't." Shirlee picks at the hem of her T-shirt, finding a loose thread and winding it around her finger. "I can barely breathe when she's around."

"You have to stand up to her. It's the only way to shut her down. That's how it works with bullies."

She winds the thread tighter, turning the end of her finger white.

"One of the few advantages of going to so many schools is you see lots of bullies in action. And learn how to get them to leave you alone."

She unwinds the thread and sticks her hands in her pockets. "You're a good friend, Raine."

Really? A warmth settles in my stomach. That's a new role for me.

Shirlee slumps against my side.

If Jennifer can have this effect on Shirlee in just a couple of weeks, what did she do to Emily?

CHAPTER 12

$\mathcal{J}$t's not till Friday that Yielding Middle is populated to its max again. Avalon's still absent, though. That girl is so skinny, she can't afford to have the stomach flu for days.

It's the usual routine at the beginning of cross-country practice. Everyone hustles out to the field to warm up. Well, everyone except Jennifer and Alyssa. They saunter down the hall to fill their water bottles under the false impression they're special and don't need to hurry. It's easy to time it so I'm briefly alone in the locker room.

Jennifer's necklace hangs from a locker hook, the supernova sparkle glinting from the stone. I want that memory. I want to take it home and spend some serious time with it. Any memory shining its guts out like that must have something to say.

As quick as a fly zipping through a closing door, I snatch Jennifer's combination lock from where it's lying on the bench and shove it to the back of my locker. Then I shut my locker door, throw on my lock, and dash around the corner. Out of sight, I stand by the door that leads outside, listening.

Alyssa and Jennifer make their way back to the locker area.

"Alyssa, do you have my lock?" Jennifer asks.

"What would I do with two locks?" Alyssa says.

"I don't know, but I can't find it anywhere."

"Yeah, because you've got the messiest locker in the school," Alyssa says. "Just close your locker door."

I slip out quietly, join the others on the grass, and begin stretching.

"Hurry up, girls," Coach yells when Jennifer and Alyssa finally emerge from the locker room. "It's a street run today, and that's a longer workout."

The whole time my feet are pounding the pavement, I'm thinking through how I need to snatch the necklace while Jennifer and everyone else are in the showers. Getting caught would be bad. Getting caught would make me Jennifer's main target. And life doesn't get any suckier than being the mean girl's main target.

We're cooling down when Willow jogs up next to me. "You hear about Avalon?" she asks.

"No," I say. "What happened?"

"She got the flu so bad, she ended up dehydrated. Her mom took her to the hospital last night, and they put her on an IV."

I imagine Avalon all wizened and brittle like an apple chip. "She's going to be okay?"

"Yeah, she's already home." Willow swipes her arm across her sweaty forehead. "She'll be back in school on Monday."

The second we enter the change room, my eyes cut to Jennifer. She opens the door of her locker and a brush falls out. The necklace swings gently from the hook, its sparkle practically blinding me.

"Raine? Raine?" Willow says. She pokes me in the shoulder.

"Huh?"

"I was asking about the language arts homework. Did you get it written down?"

"Yeah."

"Can I see it? I missed the last two questions." Willow unzips her backpack and pulls out a notebook.

Jennifer's gathering up her shower stuff. "Alyssa, you sure you don't have my lock?"

"I don't have it." Alyssa slips on flip-flops. "Hurry up. My mom said we absolutely can't be late today."

Jennifer and Alyssa head to the showers.

I quickly dial the combo to open my lock. "I have a dentist appointment." I hand Willow my language arts notebook. "In like forty minutes. I don't even have time for a shower."

"Eww," Torie says.

"I'll be fast." Willow sits down on the bench.

I get dressed. On my way out, I make a point of telling a few girls goodbye, mentioning my dentist appointment.

I wait outside the building, around the corner from the gym door. I count under my breath, in time with my heart, which is launching itself against my rib cage. By one hundred, the girls should be in the showers. I hope.

. . . ninety-eight . . . ninety-nine . . . one hundred.

I reenter the locker room.

It's empty. In one breath, I fly across the room. Glance around. Still no one. I tug open Jennifer's locker. I pull her lock from my pocket and shove it in her shoe at the back of the space. My hand darts in again and seizes the necklace.

Score.

I arrive home to a dog anxious for a walk. "Levi, I promise I'll take you out later. For now, please just run around the yard." After ten minutes, I call her in, give her a biscuit, then go upstairs.

Sitting cross-legged on my bed, I hold Jennifer's necklace in the air by the clasp. The stone dangles and spins, the sparkle flashing and dancing. My fingers tingle, full of electricity.

Maybe I'll find a memory that'll help Shirlee get Jennifer off her back. Or one about Emily. Or maybe I'll pick up a bunch of memories.

I squeeze the stone in my palm. I shut my eyes.

Nothing.

I blow out an impatient breath. The stone definitely has a memory. Or memories. But how do I access them?

If only my grandmother were still alive. She was a genius at this. She could even tease a vision from an object without a sparkle.

We thought we'd have years and years together for her to teach me. Then one evening, she went out to water the garden. I waited for her to tuck me in. Waited and waited, flipping through picture book after picture book. Eventually, our neighbor came to the door. My grandmother had had a huge heart attack and was gone.

I try to think of memory things she mentioned. Around the time I started kindergarten, a friend of hers, someone else who could pull visions from objects, came for dinner.

I remember them sitting at the kitchen table. A big pot of hot soup was in the middle of the table, the steam from it curling up like magic.

My grandmother pushed back her chair and stood. "Let me show you." She disappeared into the pantry and returned with an onion.

"I peel away the memories as if I'm peeling an onion," she explained. Her hands were in the air, moving in and out of the steam. "From the most recent to the oldest memory." She peeled off a layer. "So this could be from yesterday." She peeled off the next layer. "And now I've uncovered a memory from last week." She removed yet another layer. "And here's one from a month ago."

Excited, I grip the necklace again. How incredible would that be, to unlock memories going back in time? It's never happened for me. Never. I'm basically a toddler in the world of memory gathering. Just learning to talk and walk.

I think of an onion as clearly as I can, crackly skin tearing off to reveal the paper-white skin that stings your eyes.

Nothing.

I focus on the tingles.

Nothing.

I imagine Jennifer in class. At lunch. Running.

Nothing, nothing, nothing.

In disgust, I toss the necklace on my dresser, where it rolls next to my phone.

"This is not working, Levi." I go down to the kitchen for a glass of milk and some cookies. Levi pads after me, whining a little to remind me I promised her a walk.

Annoyed, I sit on a barstool in the semidark. The memory, possibly memories, is so close, but still out of reach. Suddenly a thought lights up my brain. My grandmother was into cooking, so the onion idea worked for her. Maybe I need to try this my way, use what I'm into to uncover the memories.

Carrying a candle warmer and a votive, I go back to my room. I set a wax melt in the pan of the warmer and light the votive. The melting cube gives off the sweet scent of sugar cookies. I boot up my computer and click on my latest playlist. Music bounces off the walls. I pick up the necklace and cradle the stone in my hand.

The first memory plops into my mind as if it was just sitting there, waiting for me to show up.

It's recent—Jennifer is in a cool spaghetti-strap dress that I've seen her wear to school. She's at a store, swiping different glosses across the back of her hand.

I imagine a back key and press it.

Now she's in a kitchen, yelling at a woman about how the shirt she wants to wear is still in dirty laundry. It's the woman in the black car who checked that I was going to clean up after Levi. Jennifer's mother.

I keep hanging on to the necklace, pressing the imaginary back key, rewinding time by baby steps.

Press. Press. Press.

Until finally, I hit pay dirt.

Jennifer, Alyssa, and Danielle are clearing off a coffee table, moving gossip magazines, loose papers, a couple of remotes, and a container of Legos to the floor. Then they cover the table with nail stuff and snacks.

"We gotta do something to Emily." Jennifer sits on a cushion on the floor and vigorously shakes a bottle of polish. "She can't go after Michael and get away with it."

"Like he'd ever be interested in her. She's beyond gross." Alyssa kneels and dips her fingers in a bowl of sudsy water. "The way she stinks like old cabbage, the way she clicks her

tongue when she's thinking and spit gets on her lips. The way she dresses. Ugh."

"Emily makes me want to throw up. And it's not like I have a sensitive gag reflex." Danielle lays her hand flat on the table in front of Jennifer. "It's worth it to me to fail math. Just so I don't have to deal with her anymore."

"We need a plan." Jennifer unscrews the cap of the bottle. "To punish her."

The girls are quiet, thinking.

"Let's ditch her somewhere," Jennifer says slowly. "I mean really ditch her."

"She deserves it," Danielle says.

"Isn't she afraid of the dark?" Alyssa pulls her fingers out of the water, pushes back the cuticles with a plastic utensil, then submerges them again.

"We'll leave her somewhere dark." Jennifer brushes bright turquoise on Danielle's nails. "And really freak her out."

"I know the perfect place." Danielle's eyes light up. "Off Highway Twenty. My dad took me hiking there last year. Super backwoods. No lights. No buildings. No cell service."

"Where exactly is it?" Jennifer asks, the brush suspended in midair.

"You know the hotel sign?"

"I know where you're talking about." Alyssa nods. "Isn't there a bridge? At least, there used to be."

"Still is," Danielle says. "At the top of the ravine."

"We'll do it next Saturday when my parents are out of town

for the weekend," Jennifer says. "We can have a sleepover. I'll invite Emily."

"Are my cuticles done?" Alyssa holds her hands out for the others to check.

Danielle nods.

"First she can do my project, and then we'll make her so sorry she ever came to Yielding," Jennifer says, staring across the room, her eyes cold and mean.

CHAPTER 13

*M*y mom goes to work on Saturday—weekends are prime renting time. So I'm kicking around the house, jotting down ideas for my project with Hugh, and watching TV.

Around noon, my phone flashes with a text from Torie:

Mall with me, Sydney, and Willow? My mom's driving.

Am I actually making friends?

Sure, I reply.

A minivan pulls into the driveway thirty minutes later, and the door slides open. I climb into the empty spot in the middle seat with Willow and Sydney. My fingers immediately start tingling. The van's probably loaded with sparkles, although I'm not seeing any. I squint. One on Willow's earring and one on Sydney's phone. I sit on my hands. I will not look weird today.

Everyone says hi.

"Nice to meet you, Raine," Torie's mom says. "Thanks for helping support Torie's sister."

What?

Torie turns around from the front seat. "My sister starts a new job today at the henna tattoo kiosk. My mom wants her to look all popular, so we have to hang around the booth for a while and get tattoos."

A henna tattoo? How much does that cost? I barely have any money.

"I'm paying for your tattoos, girls." It's as if Torie's mom read my mind. "After all, you're doing our family a huge favor."

"She gets paid by the number of tattoos she does," Torie explains.

"I've seen some of Turner's designs," Willow offers. "They're adorable."

"My mom said I should get mine on the back of my hand." Sydney looks up from the game she's playing on her phone.

"We'll all get them on our hands. Same hand. Same design," Torie announces. "Like we're a club."

And what started off sounding like a sketchy plan,

before Torie gave me the whole story, ends up sounding kind of wacky and fun and like I'm included in something.

When we arrive at the mall, Torie's mom gives her money for our tattoos, then leaves us to go chat with some lady she knows.

"My mom contacted everyone to show up here today." Torie shakes her head. "Let's get in line. There are other things I want to do today besides get a tattoo from my sister. Like she hasn't been practicing on me at home, anyway."

"I desperately need new mascara," Sydney says. "Mine's all dried up."

Torie points to her hair. "And I need some new color. This blue is already fading."

There's a long list of things I need, too. The problem is that money's the number one item.

I haven't been to a mall in ages, and I'd forgotten how my hands go crazy with tingling. If I could see all the sparkles around, I bet it'd look like a diamond mine.

"Hey, Hannah." Torie taps the shoulder of the girl in front of us.

The girl squeals and hugs Torie. "How's your team doing this year?" she asks, not even bothering to say hi.

"Great. We're doing great," Torie says with a tinge of annoyance. "This is my cousin Hannah. She goes to Carlton Oaks Middle." She nods at each of us in turn. "This is Sydney, Willow, and Raine."

"You guys do cross-country?" Hannah asks.

"Yeah, they're on my team," Torie says, sounding more annoyed.

"We are so going to pound your butts this season. Our coach has been working us extra hard." As the line moves, Hannah walks backward so she still faces us.

Sydney crosses her arms.

"They barely beat us last year," Willow whispers in my ear. "Hannah always has to be better than Torie at everything."

If cousins are this irritating maybe I'm better off not having any.

"We've been training hard, too," Torie says. "Plus, Raine's new. And she's crazy fast."

Hannah looks me up and down. "Where're you from?"

"Detroit," I say.

"Hannah," Torie says, "you won't believe where Raine lives. In Emily Huvar's old house."

Hannah knows Emily?

"Emily went to Hannah's school before she transferred to Yielding Middle last fall," Torie explains.

"You knew her?" I ask Hannah.

"Yeah. Not as a friend or anything. But yeah, I knew her," Hannah says. "That's such a sad story."

We all nod.

"Not like she had a happy time at my school, but at least she didn't die," she continues.

My ears prick up. "What do you mean?"

"She was big-time bullied. Like once, these girls locked

her in a closet in the art room. She was in there for hours. Until the custodian let her out." Hannah pulls her hair up in a ponytail, then lets it drop. "Her parents transferred her after that."

"That's horrible," Willow says, her face scrunched up like she's imagining it.

Was Emily bullied everywhere she went?

"She didn't change schools because her family moved?" I ask. I guess I assumed her scenario was the same as mine.

"Other way around," Hannah says. "She changed schools to get a new start. Her family moved to Yielding so they'd be close to Emily's new school."

"She was picked on at our school, too," Willow says sadly.

"By Jennifer and those guys," Sydney says to me.

A couple of girls wander past us, holding out their arms. I glance at their tattoos. The lines are kind of wobbly and smudged. How good is Torie's sister?

"Is Turner any good at henna tattoos?" Sydney asks, her eyes on the same girls I'm watching.

"No," Torie says cheerfully. "She sucks."

"That's what I heard, too," Hannah says. "Remember when she tried working at the ceramics place? My mug cracked in half the first time I used it."

"That job was such a disaster," Torie says. The two girls laugh.

"Did Emily go to a lot of sleepovers at Jennifer's?" I ask.

Torie shrugs. "I doubt it. Emily was doing Jennifer's

homework. The sleepover was probably 'payment' for the big project we had." She makes air quotes around *payment*.

Exactly what I thought after the diorama vision.

"Besides, Emily was pretty bizarre," Sydney says. "I bet she didn't get many invitations for anything."

"We shouldn't say negative things about her," Willow says.

There's a short silence.

"Emily had a reputation for being a computer genius," Hannah says. "She even knew more than the computer teacher. Emily said if she wanted to, she could hack into the school records and change everyone's grades."

We've been steadily shuffling along, and now we're at the front of the line.

"I'll be the first victim," Hannah says dramatically. She presses one arm against her forehead and stretches out the other one.

When it's my turn, I sit on the stool across from Turner. Her whole face is damp with sweat. She keeps shaking her hands in the air, like they're cramping. She looks nervous and exhausted.

"Thanks," I say when she's finished.

"You're welcome." She gazes at the line behind me and sighs.

At the food court, Torie, Sydney, Willow, and I lay our hands flat on a table and compare our tattoos. They do look sort of the same, the way all humans look sort of the same. Everyone's tattoo has dark brown and reddish henna lines, some curvy, some straight, with a similar sunflower-ish design. Willow's tattoo is half the size of the others. Sydney's has thicker lines. Mine is missing several petals. Torie's looks like her sister was wearing a blindfold.

I sip my soda, thinking about how the tattoos are like sparkles. The four of us are joined together because we have the tattoos in common. Seeing someone's memory links me to that person because we have their memory in common.

Was Emily connected to anyone at school? Did she have any friends? Or was she always alone?

"What kind of big project?" I suddenly ask Torie.

"What?" she says.

"If the sleepover was payment for Emily doing Jennifer's project, what subject was the project for?"

"It was a really obnoxious chemistry project," Torie replies. "I wish someone had done mine."

"You mean when we had to make a model of a compound?" Sydney says. "I hated that project."

"Jennifer's turned out really cool," Willow says. "It was made of Lego bricks."

At the word *Lego,* I go simultaneously cold and sweaty.

Because in the memory from Jennifer's necklace, the girls moved a bucket from the coffee table to the floor. A bucket of Lego bricks. That hadn't been made into anything yet.

CHAPTER 14

I feed Levi, then text my mom to find out what time she'll be home for dinner.

When I don't hear back, a nugget of worry lodges in my chest.

I've been slacking when it comes to keeping an eye on her. Usually, I'm on hyperalert, watching for the first signs of a loser. Then I rush in and slam on the brakes. It works, sometimes. I've been to five different schools. It could've been double that.

I text again. Radio silence.

My mom falls into relationships the way other people finish a bag of chips zoned out in front of the TV. It happens when she's not paying attention. A guy who stays late at work to help her can easily morph into a guy who parks his razor on our bathroom counter and his feet on our coffee table for Saturday-night hockey.

I text again. By now, a weight the size of my social studies textbook presses on my chest, making it tough to breathe. I try to remember. How many times has she come home late? Has she been getting lots of texts? Are her eyes all bright when she talks about a certain guy? Is she mentioning one guy's name too much?

I'm practically hyperventilating, imagining us repacking and loading up the truck, when I hear the crunch of tires on our driveway. My mom breezes in, clutching a brown paper bag.

"I texted you," I blurt out.

"You did?" She frowns. She sets the bag on the counter and pulls her phone from her purse. "Sorry. I put my phone on vibrate for a meeting and never switched it back to ring."

The weight lifts a little, and I suck in a decent breath.

My mom opens the bag, and our little kitchen fills with yummy smells. "Greek," she says. "From this restaurant called Athens near the apartments in Oneida."

She pulls out a salad, hummus, pita bread, a gyro, a chicken shish kebob and two flower-shaped baklavas. I get glasses of water, and we sit at the counter to eat.

"Henna tattoo?" she asks, pointing a plastic fork at my hand.

"This girl at school's sister does them at the mall."

My mom tilts her head to look at the tattoo from different angles.

"It's supposed to be a sunflower," I say.

My mom chatters about work. She describes this gross-sounding complex they're fixing up to rent. I hang on every word, analyzing, scrutinizing, looking for clues that she's interested in someone. Nothing.

"How's the unpacking going?" I ask as I pop the last bite of baklava into my mouth. When my mother starts falling in love, she stops unpacking. Actually, she stops doing everything except hanging out with the guy.

"Come see my room." My mom stands.

I walk into her bedroom and gasp. Literally gasp. Only three boxes are piled in the corner, still waiting to be emptied. Three. I can't even remember the last time my mother unpacked this much. Brass knickknacks in the shape of animals are lined up on the shelf behind her bed. I haven't seen them in years. A few pictures hang on the wall. A little doily sits under her alarm clock.

"Wow, Mom," I say. "It's incredible."

She beams. "Although, you should see the basement. I empty a box and just toss it down the stairs. It must look like a cardboard graveyard."

I make a face.

"Don't worry. You don't have to go down there." She waves her arms, as if dismissing the thought. "I'll take care of it. Besides my boxes, I noticed a mattress and a few other odds and ends."

A mattress? I wonder if Tasha ever slept down there. Most likely not. The basement's pretty nasty. I tell my mom what our nosy old-lady neighbor said about teens sneaking into our house and getting up to stuff.

"I believe it. I've seen it happen with other vacant houses," she says, straightening a small brass horse. "The neighbor's name is Mrs. Burns, by the way."

"You met her?" I ask.

"I think she makes it a point to talk to everyone on the street." My mom smiles. "She sees herself as the ears and eyes of the neighborhood."

"You know who snuck past Mrs. Burns?" I pause. "Tasha, the little sister of the girl who disappeared. She came in our back door with a key the day I was home sick," I say. "She had her lunch with her."

My mom sighs, and her lips and eyes turn down in sadness. She has a soft spot the size of New York for anyone going through tough times. "That poor girl. Her life will never be the same."

There's silence while we're both probably thinking about how life can take a turn for the worse.

"I really am trying, Raine," my mom says quietly. "This is the fresh start that will stick."

A flutter of hope flits through me. I hope she's right.

After my mom goes to bed, I sit outside in the dark on the porch. There's no moon or stars tonight. I pull up the hood of my sweatshirt in the chilly breeze. A small animal rustles on the ground nearby. The night wraps around me until I feel completely alone.

Was it this dark and quiet in the woods where Emily got left? How alone did she feel? How scared? I shiver like a thousand spiders are skittering all over me.

I take Jennifer's necklace from my pouch pocket. The sparkle on the stone flashes, cutting through the inky gloom. I cradle the necklace in my palm.

Shutting my eyes, I go straight to the memory of the girls doing their nails and plotting to leave Emily in the forest. I guess my mind remembers the path.

Zooming in on the papers the girls cleared off the coffee table, I find the instructions for the science project.

FINAL 7TH GRADE CHEMISTRY PROJECT

Due June 23

Using common household materials, construct a compound of your choice.

I stop reading and switch my focus to the bucket of Legos. Emily snapped these little bricks together into a compound for Jennifer. This is the science project Emily mentioned to Hugh when they met on the night she vanished.

Emily didn't disappear on the way to Jennifer's sleepover. There was no bad guy.

Just three very mean girls.

Who made her do a chemistry project.

Then took her to a secluded place in the woods and left her.

What happened out there?

Something so bad that Alyssa's hand shook when she found out where I lived. Something so bad that Alyssa lost her balance when she heard the police might go hard-core with the investigation again. Something so bad that Emily didn't make it back to Yielding.

Jennifer, Alyssa, and Danielle took Emily out into the forest and left her.

Did she die there?

CHAPTER 15

*A*valon's back at school on Monday, all over Hugh like a wet T-shirt.

When I pass them in the hall, Hugh waves to me. "We still on for Thursday at the Bean? Six-thirty, right?"

Avalon inches closer to him. How is this even physically possible?

"Yeah," I reply.

"I haven't done any work yet, but I will." Hugh raises three fingers. "Scout's honor."

Avalon is frowning, a deep line etched across her narrow forehead. Apparently, she's not pleased with the partner arrangement for film.

At lunch I sit with Torie, Sydney, Willow, and a few other cross-country girls.

"Check this out." Torie slaps her tattooed hand on the table.

Sydney does the same. Then Willow does, and finally, so do I.

Next we walk our fingers along the table, doing little leaps and turns and the cancan. We're a henna hand dance routine.

"Cool," says the girl next to me. "Are those tattoos real?"

"Real henna," Torie says.

"I like how they're all different," another girl says.

We break out laughing.

Shirlee's standing awkwardly at the end of the table.

"Sit, Shirlee," I say, scooting along the bench. "There's room."

She looks wistfully at our hands.

That's where I have an advantage over her. It's easier to make friends at a new school when you're on a team. I know she's in the Spanish club, but they don't eat together.

I'm finishing up my cookies when Jennifer, Alyssa, and Danielle come striding down the aisle toward us.

Shirlee folds into herself like she's trying to disappear origami-style.

A storm brews in my stomach. The necklace is in my backpack, which is in my locker. Right before practice today, I'm going to shove it to the very back of Jennifer's locker. Luckily, there's no PE class last period, so the locker room will be empty, with no one to discover the necklace by accident and take it for themselves. There's a slim, mostly nonexistent chance Jennifer will think she just didn't find it at the end of Friday's practice because of how far back on the shelf I'll put it. Most importantly, she'll have no way of linking me to the necklace. Being tossed in a pit of spiders would be more pleasant than what she would do to me if she found out.

Jennifer and her girls stand side by side, hands on hips, at the end of our table. Jennifer looks naked without her necklace and the big sparkle that was glommed onto it.

"Where's my necklace?" She glares at me.

"What?" I say, trying to look confused. Meanwhile, it feels as though someone's twisting up my guts and wringing them out like they're a rag.

"You were in the locker room on Friday when it disappeared." Her eyebrows are raised to her hairline.

"Are you actually accusing me of stealing your necklace?" I tilt my head and scowl, acting like a girl who routinely jumps into lunchtime brawls.

"Raine left early for a dentist appointment that day," Torie says, her elbows on the table, her chin resting on her hands, tattooed hand on top. "She didn't even take a shower."

"It's Juicy jewelry." Jennifer looks me over, like she's assigning rock-bottom price tags to each item I'm wearing. "That probably doesn't mean anything to you."

"Raine wasn't there when your necklace went missing," Torie insists.

Sydney and Willow stare with large, round eyes from Jennifer to me to Torie. Shirlee's chewing on her bottom lip. Everyone else is gazing at the table, like the secrets of the universe are etched in the Formica.

"Let's go." Alyssa links her arm through Jennifer's, and Danielle takes the other arm. The three sashay away from us.

"Thanks," I say to Torie.

"No prob," she says, punching a fist in the air. "Henna girls unite."

The end-of-lunch buzzer rings.

"That necklace is probably super expensive," Shirlee says as we're walking out.

"I saw it at Budget Mart for a dollar ninety-nine," I say, continuing with my tough-girl act even though I'm shaking inside.

Shirlee laughs nervously. "Be careful, Raine. You know how awful she can be."

I think of Emily, excited and babbling to Hugh about the sleepover, then ending up in the dark woods, and then who knows what. "Yeah, I do."

A black fog of dread surrounds me all afternoon. The necklace is in a small pocket in my backpack, but it might as well be wound around my neck, pulling tighter and tighter. It sparkles and shines, but it's like a curse. I can't wait to get rid of it and never touch it again.

✸

"The periodic table gives me a headache," Willow complains as we leave science. "Even after Mrs. Woodford went over the entire worksheet my head was still in an electron cloud. And I'm not trying to be funny."

I didn't hear a word the teacher said.

"You're so pale." Willow's eyebrows bunch together in worry. "Is it about Jennifer?"

I shrug.

"Don't let her get to you," Willow says. "I'm sure after what Torie said she knows you didn't take her necklace."

Sweat beads over my entire body. I give a half nod.

"I feel sorry for the person who did take it." Willow shudders. "You should've seen her, tearing up the locker room, yelling at everyone, calling us names. It was like she was rabid."

"I'm glad I missed it," I say, feeling sick.

Willow points. "What's going on?"

The classroom door to film is closed, and the entire class is milling around in the hall.

"Stupid sub," Torie says when we get within talking distance. "She won't let us in till she's finished reading a chapter. She has another dumb test tonight."

"She can do that?" I ask.

"It's not like anyone's racing to the office to report her." Sydney shoots a look at Torie. "I'm personally okay with a little free time."

"Party in the hall." Garrett dances around.

Jennifer's necklace is sending my anxiety level off the charts. And with the entire class in the hall, my fingers are freaking out with tingles.

When Garrett passes me, I snag a sparkle off his binder. I can't help myself. I also can't read it, but at least holding a sparkle numbs the tingling.

Hugh and Avalon are sitting cross-legged on the floor, playing video games on their phones. It's the first time I've seen her smiling and doing something other than hang off him.

Shirlee and her partner for the project, a slender guy with acne, are leaning against the wall, taking notes.

Now would be the perfect time to sneak off to the locker room and dump the necklace. It may not look heavy, but it's weighing down my backpack like a hundred bricks.

Out of the corner of my eye, I catch movement. The way a gazelle sees starving lions padding toward her.

I step away.

Too late. Jennifer, Alyssa, and Danielle elbow past Torie and Willow. Jennifer yanks my backpack off my shoulders.

She drops it on the ground.

"Hey, what are you doing?" Torie says loudly.

That gets everyone's attention. Several people drift over and surround us. I think I'm going to suffocate.

"Raine has something of mine," Jennifer says, roughly pulling on the zipper to my backpack's main compartment. "Help me," she barks at Alyssa and Danielle.

Alyssa dumps the contents out. Books thud on the

linoleum. Loose papers flutter away like snowflakes. My binder splats open.

It's a nightmare in slow motion. I stand frozen, trying to get my legs, my lips, anything to work.

Torie's mouth opens and shuts, telling the girls to stop. They ignore her.

Danielle pulls out my water bottle and sends it rolling down the hall.

Shirlee bends over to retrieve it.

Danielle starts unzipping the pouches at the front of my backpack.

My breath snags in my throat.

Jennifer glances at the still-closed classroom door. "Hurry up."

Danielle sticks in a hand and grabs my thumb drive, calculator, pens, pencils, and highlighters from the largest pouch. She drops them to the floor.

My throat narrows.

Alyssa kneels and unzips the next compartment. She tosses out my tampons and extra lunch money.

With jerky, impatient movements, Jennifer grabs my backpack. She begins yanking the zipper of the smallest pocket, the last remaining compartment, the pocket holding her necklace.

It takes two seconds. It takes two years. The hall is noisy. The hall is quiet. I'm hot. I'm freezing.

Hugh finally tunes in and joins the crowd. "Give Raine her backpack, Jennifer," he says. "Don't be a jerk."

But he's too late to be my knight in shining armor.

Jennifer beams a cruel smile, like it was sliced into her face with a knife. Link by link, she gently tugs the chain from the pocket until the entire necklace emerges, shiny, glimmering, winking at everyone. "I knew it was in here," she says triumphantly.

Jennifer stands, dangling the necklace by my head like it's an Olympic medal. "KleptoRainia."

Torie's hands are shoved in her pockets, the henna tattoo hidden. Hugh looks shocked. Shirlee has tears in her eyes.

I run down the hall and out the first door I come to.

CHAPTER 16

$\mathcal{M}$y mom arrives home from work around six. "Raine?" she calls upstairs. "It was someone's birthday in the office. I brought home leftover cake."

When I get to the kitchen, she's already digging in.

"Corner pieces," she says, perching on a barstool. "Let's eat dinner backward and start with dessert."

The cake would plug up my throat and choke me to death.

"It's time to leave Yielding." My voice cracks. I'm on the verge of losing it.

"What?" Her fork jerks to a stop, and a little cake topples to the counter. "You've been crying. What's going on?"

I don't answer. I learned years ago that it's either useless or dangerous to give my mom too much info. Because she'll either (a) do nothing to help or (b) go way overboard. When I was in third grade, a boy accused me of pulling his hair. Not true. I was reaching for a sparkle on the top of his head. Weirdest thing, but the sparkle was sticky. Anyway, the teacher called home to discuss my behavior. Would my mom let it go with a simple "I'll talk to Raine"? No, she made a huge deal of it, even going to the principal about how the teacher singled me out. The upshot was no one would let their kid play with me. Loneliest year of my life.

"What happened?" she asks.

"I don't want to talk about it."

"You're sure it's that bad?" Mom says in a calm voice. "You know how middle school works. The first few days might be rough, but then the next drama will come along."

"We have to move." I walk over to the cupboard and start pulling down dishes and stacking them on the counter. Leaving's the only logical solution. Moving is what we do. I certainly can't go back to Yielding Middle. Ever.

She watches in silence, massaging her forehead where a blue vein pulses.

By the time I start with the glasses and mugs, I'm actually feeling better. Like I've been transported to the moon, where I'm light and weightless.

"I am so ready for a fresh start." I practically sing the last two words. I never realized how sweet they sound. Sweeter than cake. *Fresh start.* I finally understand why my mother was always so quick to load up the truck and stick the key in the ignition.

When I start stacking silverware and cooking utensils and everything else from the kitchen drawers on the counter, she walks over and wraps her arms around me. "Raine." She holds me close. "We haven't even been here a month. My job's going well. You're going to have to face the music on this one," she says softly. "Whatever it is."

I step back from her, anger flaring inside me. "Why? Why do I have to face the music? When did *you* ever face the music, Mom? Oh yeah, that would be never. We're constantly moving so you can get away from some loser. We've left a guy behind in every place I can remember since I came to live with you." My voice gets louder. "*You* should try facing the music."

The bluish vein on my mom's temple pulses fast, like a hummingbird's wings.

I know I should stop, but I can't. "Like, why'd we just leave Detroit? Because you hooked up with a guy who stole from us. We bought our stuff back from the pawnshop and then what? We ran away."

My mom opens her mouth, but no words come out.

"It's *my* turn for a fresh start!" I yell. "*My* turn."

Slowly, she shakes her head.

I pick up a plate and hurl it across the room. It hits the wall with a loud crash, raining smashed pieces onto the floor.

My fingers curl around the next plate. For a second, I think about throwing all the plates, one by one. Then I take a deep shuddery breath and escape to my room.

From my bed, I hear my mother downstairs sweeping up the broken pieces. And then I hear a knock at the door.

"Hi. My name's Shirlee. I have Raine's backpack."

"Thank you," my mom says. She must be wondering what's next. First I won't give up details about what went down at school. Then I'm flinging plates at walls. And then a girl she's never met shows up with my backpack.

"Would it be possible for me to talk to Raine?" Shirlee asks.

There's a brief silence. My mom's trying to decide if her screaming, plate-throwing, secret-keeping daughter wants to talk to Shirlee.

"How's she doing?" Shirlee asks, sounding genuinely concerned.

"Not great," my mom admits. "I don't think I've ever seen her this upset."

"I might be able to make her feel a little better," Shirlee offers.

"Come in," my mom says. "I'll see if she's up for a visitor."

When my mom pokes her head in my room, I slip past her and down the stairs. I'm not talking to her.

"Thanks," I say to Shirlee, gesturing at the backpack.

"No problem. I hope I got everything."

I lift my shoulders. What am I supposed to say? Yeah, I hope you got all my belongings, including the tampons, from where they were tossed up and down the hall during the most humiliating experience of my life?

"You ever been to Grinders?" Shirlee asks. "It's not very popular, but they have great hot chocolate."

"Let's go," I say, keying in on the *not very popular*— meaning we won't bump into anyone from school. Plus, I need time away from my mother.

At the bottom of the driveway, we veer left. There's a sparkle on Shirlee's purse strap, but I'm too worn out to even be interested in it. Maybe I have to be an emotional basket case for sparkles not to tempt me. That sounds like a fun life.

"Grinders is kind of a hole-in-the-wall. Just to warn you. And it's more of an old people's hangout." She takes a moment to push her long hair over her shoulder. "I haven't told my mom about my problems with Jennifer. It's too embarrassing. I wasn't sure how much you wanted me to say about today at your house."

"I didn't tell my mom, either."

"Some people think Jennifer planted her necklace in your backpack," Shirlee says. "And that Alyssa and Danielle were in on it."

"Why would they do that?"

"They don't need a reason. And Jennifer's merciless when it comes to new girls." She cringes.

I think of the plan they cooked up for Emily. All because Jennifer wanted to teach her a lesson. And I think of Shirlee in the school bathroom.

"A couple of people—well, mostly Torie—think you and your mom travel around the country, collecting items to sell to the pawnshop in Las Vegas, the one that's on TV."

"That's just crazy." I actually laugh a little, which surprises me because I didn't think I'd find anything to laugh about for at least ten years. "Although I wouldn't mind seeing that pawnshop."

"That'd be cool."

"Any other theories?" What does Hugh think?

"Some people think you took the necklace because of the way your hands—" She presses her lips so tightly together, they turn white.

I feel my face flame. They mean the way my hands are always fluttering and reaching out. I try to keep them still, but it's like they take on a life of their own when sparkles are around.

We walk in silence for a few minutes.

"This way." Shirlee turns into the drive of a tiny strip mall with a skateboard store, a nail salon, and a sushi restaurant. Grinders is at the back, not visible from the street.

She holds the door for me. It's small inside, with four booths along the wall and two round tables with chairs in the middle of the room. Most seats are taken by customers chatting and playing board games. From the back corner, a jukebox belts out old-people music. I see right away what Shirlee meant. It's a gray-haired crowd. And they're all talking to each other in loud voices. It smells of coffee and cookies.

There are several sparkles, and my fingers tingle.

"Shirlee," says the old man behind the counter. "You brought a friend."

"Raine, Bert. Bert, Raine." Shirlee waves the introductions. "Bert's been working here for decades. Literally."

"It's true," he says. "Haven't updated my resume in forty years."

"That might be something for the Guinness World Records book," I say.

"Two hot chocolates? Extra whipped cream?" he asks.

"Sounds good." Shirlee looks at me, a question in her eyes.

"Sure," I say.

We sit at the first booth, the only empty booth.

"Do they have Wi-Fi here?" I ask Shirlee.

"No, but you can pick it up from the nail salon. It's not password-protected."

I'm thinking I'll come here for Wi-Fi. I'm never showing my face at the Bean again.

Bert hobbles over with our drinks and a plate of sugar cookies. "The cookies are on the house."

"Thanks," Shirlee and I say simultaneously.

I sip hot chocolate, then lick off my mustache. "It's nice here. Kind of homey, in an elderly way."

"Why don't you go to the principal? Tell him what the girls did to you?" With a plastic spoon, Shirlee shaves off strips of whipped cream and eats them.

"No," I say. "Things would only get worse if I did that."

"I guess they did a good job setting you up."

I dunk a cookie. More like I did a good job setting myself up. Not that I'm willing to share that thought with Shirlee.

"I had an interesting horoscope. You did, too." Shirlee scrapes off more whipped cream. "And they made me wonder: Could we take her down?"

"You mean make life miserable for Jennifer to the point she leaves us alone? And whoever else she's picking on?" Half my cookie crumbles into my mug.

"Exactly." She leans forward, waiting for my answer.

"I've never seen it done. I've seen girls ignore the mean girl and sometimes mouth off to her. Over time, it helped." I fish out bits of soggy cookie with a spoon. "But to actually take the mean girl down? That could really explode in your face."

CHAPTER 17

$\mathcal{M}$y mom and I spend the rest of the evening like two cats, prowling around silently, careful not to cross paths. When she's watching TV in the living room, I hit up the kitchen for food. When I'm in the shower, she grabs something to eat.

She goes to work Tuesday. I call the absence line, fake my mom's voice, then skip school and watch TV all day in my pajamas. Late in the afternoon, I finally drag myself to the shower and try to scrub off the tattoo. I doubt Torie, Sydney, and Willow want me in the henna tattoo gang anymore. Well, maybe Willow does. She's so nice, she probably doesn't even kill flies or mosquitoes or cockroaches.

Later that night, when I'm already in bed but not asleep,

Mom pushes open the door to my room and tiptoes to the middle. She stands in a moonbeam, surrounded by pearly light.

"Raine, you don't want to be like me." Her voice is sad. "Running away every time life gets tricky."

I sit up, my legs dangling over the edge of the frame.

"It's too bad your grandmother died. Your life would've been a lot better, a lot more stable, I guess." She stands there quietly, her arms hanging limply at her sides. "Look, I didn't realize until this weekend what I was doing. What kind of role model I've been." She closes her eyes briefly. "It's not okay to take off every time life gets rough."

"What are you saying?"

She straightens her shoulders. "We're doing it the right way this time. We're staying in Yielding. We'll handle whatever it was that happened at school."

"And when something goes wrong with your next boyfriend?" I ask. "What are we doing then?"

"We'll stay." She blows out a breath. "For the first time in my life, I won't run."

After she leaves, I lie on my side, watching the dust particles in the moonbeam. They float, sometimes colliding with each other, sometimes gliding past, sometimes switching directions and joining up with other particles. Whichever path they choose, the particles keep on floating. They're like people, and the moonbeam is Yielding. One of these particles is me. One is Jennifer. One is Shirlee. One is Hugh. There used to be one named Emily.

In the morning, I make another call to the absence line. Obviously I can't skip school forever with bogus illnesses. But I'm not ready to go back yet.

I head over to Grinders. Bert's sitting at a table with a few of his cronies, watching bowling on TV. He leans on a cane to get upright and limps to the counter.

"Same order?" he says. He doesn't ask why I'm not in school. Maybe he doesn't realize it's a school day. Or maybe he thinks I'm homeschooled. Or maybe he knows that sometimes it's safer to ditch.

"Yeah." I wait for him to make the hot chocolate and carry it over to the same booth Shirlee and I sat in before. I pull my laptop from its bag and power it on.

Bert rejoins his buddies. While he was filling my order, one of the men changed the TV to *The Price Is Right*. Now they're all calling out amounts and making fun of each other. From their comments, I can tell they've been friends for years and years. I'm a little jealous.

Despite Mom's brave speech, we won't settle here. She'll crack. The next loser just hasn't shown up in her life yet. My mom's got the moving gene. And she passed it on to me. Maybe taking off every time things go south isn't the best strategy, but it's our strategy. Besides, after the necklace incident, I don't want to stay here. Or do I?

Pulling up a satellite app, I scour the outskirts of Yielding. From the memory on Jennifer's necklace, I know I'm looking for a hotel sign on Highway 20. I search for one within a two-mile radius of Jennifer's house.

The girls had to somehow get to the remote area, then get back to town, which is why I'm not checking too far out. Maybe an adult or older sibling drove them, but I doubt it. Probably only Jennifer, Alyssa, and Danielle know Emily made it to the sleepover and know about ditching her. A parent or sibling would've come forward and talked to the police.

I'm coming up with nothing, so I broaden my search to three, then four, then as far away as five miles from Jennifer's.

Score. A Motel 6 sign on stilts towers over the side of a highway. When I zoom in, I find the wooden bridge the girls mentioned. The place looks deserted, with nothing but trees, bushes, rocks, and fallen leaves. And more trees. I map it from my house.

I down my hot chocolate and carry the empty mug over to the plastic bucket for dirty dishes at the back of the room. After paying Bert, I head home to grab Levi.

Together we jog the five miles to the motel sign. Next to it is a narrow, overgrown path. Tall trees stand guard over the area, letting in pointed slants of sunlight. The air is thick and humid with a woodsy, rotting smell. The only sounds are my heavy breathing, the tinkle of Levi's metal tag against her collar, and our footsteps.

The whole time we're walking, I keep my eyes peeled for a sparkle. I see nothing, and my fingertips are completely calm and quiet.

At the top of the steep hill, we reach a flat patch of dirt

and the bridge. Two birds chirp from treetops, probably asking each other what we're doing up here, in the middle of nowhere. There's not a single sign of another human. I check my phone. No service.

"Not to creep you out, Levi," I say, "but if something happens to us, no one will ever know." I shiver.

We trudge through a carpet of dead leaves to the bridge. It's a narrow suspension bridge with wooden planks and a thick rope on each side for railings, a little longer than a football field. Below the bridge? A deep ravine of sudden death.

I picture my grandmother and how she'd gaze briefly across the room and lightly twitch her fingers, as if finding a memory took more than one sense.

I stare across the bridge, keeping my eyes wide open, not blinking. I make my mind go blank. I thrust out my arms, letting my fingers dangle. I keep staring, staring until everything goes blurry: the bridge, the trees, the ground. My eyes water. And my fingertips barely begin to tingle; I feel just a few tiny pinpricks.

I blink.

The tingling disappears.

I start over, forcing my eyes to stay open in this staring contest against no one. My fingers tingle. I keep looking at the bridge but not focusing.

And then I see it.

CHAPTER 18

$\mathcal{A}$n actual sparkle twinkles on the rope railing at about the halfway point. It's huge, about the size of my head and halogen bright. I can't believe it was ever invisible.

Someone, maybe Emily, walked out there and left behind a memory.

I step onto the first plank, arms outstretched, each hand grasping a rope.

Levi whines at me.

"Quiet, Levi," I snap, nervous and edgy.

She makes a couple more unhappy noises, then lies down, drops her chin to her paws, and fixes her eyes on me. The birds stop chattering.

In the eerie quiet, I set out across the bridge, toward the

sparkle. When I'm about a third of the way, I stupidly look down and am instantly nauseous. I grip the rope so hard, my knuckles bulge.

The bridge is in bad shape. It's not totally dangerous, but I have to be careful. The rope's fraying in places. Some of the planks are starting to disintegrate. In fact, the plank right in front of me dangles like a loose tooth. I step gingerly over the gap. If it gets any worse, I'm turning back. I want the sparkle, but I'm not giving up my life for it.

I get into a rhythm: Slide right hand. Slide left hand. Shuffle right foot forward. Shuffle left foot forward. Don't look down. Repeat.

My hands are slick and sweaty, and my muscles are taut. But I'm making progress. Slowly. The sparkle twinkles at me like an expensive, exotic prize.

Suddenly a breeze kicks up. It swoops down the ravine with a vicious *whoosh.* The bridge rocks. The wood creaks like it's in pain. I scream, hanging on tight to the rope. I can't go forward. I can't go backward. I just hang on.

Levi barks from solid ground.

Just as suddenly as it arrived, the wind disappears. In the distance, I see it ruffling treetops, moving farther and farther away. The bridge slows, swinging gently, then coming to a standstill.

The sparkle shines from a few planks away.

I look over my shoulder, at the safe, solid ground where Levi gazes steadily at me.

I look at the sparkle.

It glints, bright and white, beckoning me, showing me where the memory is.

I'm going for it.

A step. Another step. I reach for it, stretching my arm out straight, locking my elbow. I grab and close my eyes.

A wedge of light from the moon slices through the dark night.

"Emily. What are you doing?" Danielle calls from the flat dirt area, panic in her voice. She lays her bike on the ground and stands, hands on hips. "It's not safe up there."

"Leave me alone!" Emily yells from the middle of the bridge.

"We came back for you," Alyssa says. "Just like we planned to."

"Get off the bridge, Emily," Danielle says.

Jennifer comes into view, wheeling a bike over the crest of the hill.

"See, Emily?" Danielle says. "Jennifer has your bike."

"Come down and ride back with us," Alyssa calls.

"What's her problem?" Jennifer jerks her head toward Emily.

"I don't know." Danielle's twisting a strand of hair. "I'm scared she's going to jump."

"She's not going to jump," Jennifer says. "She just wants attention."

Alyssa frowns. "I don't know. . . ."

"Emily, you're freaking us out," Danielle says. "Get down."

"You can pick the movie," Alyssa says.

"Leave me alone," Emily says. "Leave me alone. Leave me alone."

"She wants us to go. Let's go." Jennifer drops Emily's bike on the ground. "She can find her way home."

Danielle's twisting more strands of hair.

"You think we should leave her?" Alyssa says uncertainly.

Emily starts calling the girls names and yelling about how stupid they are. How she'll never do their homework again. And then teachers will see what idiots they really are. How they're superficial and mean.

Jennifer's face goes from annoyed to white with rage. She gestures rudely at Emily.

"You're so predictable, Jennifer. Let's see how you deal with this," Emily says to herself. Then she takes a deep breath, puffing up her chest with air, and begins to scream. Loud, high-pitched, and earsplitting.

The girls cover their ears.

When she stops, Danielle opens her mouth. "Em—"

Emily screams again.

Each time one of the girls starts to say something, Emily cuts her off with a scream.

Jennifer jerks the bike up from the ground and drags it to the edge of the ravine. "Shut up and get down or I'm throwing your bike over!" she yells to Emily. "And you can walk home by yourself in the dark."

"Don't, Jennifer," Danielle begs.

Alyssa sticks out an arm, her palm flat like a stop sign.

"Michael thinks you're pathetic, Jennifer," Emily says.

Jennifer gives the bike a rough shove.

There's silence except for the bike tumbling and toppling, crashing through bushes, smashing against rocks. It stops with a bleat of its horn, small and tinny and far, far below.

Emily screams, loud and long.

With a large arm movement, Jennifer waves to Alyssa and Danielle. Jennifer walks over the hill. Alyssa and Danielle climb onto their bikes and ride after her, the dim lights from their bikes bouncing on the uneven ground. The three girls disappear from view.

Emily screams a little longer, then suddenly stops. She tilts her head, listening, then gives one last short scream. She plops down on the bridge and pulls a water bottle from a small backpack she's wearing and gulps. She returns the water to the backpack and takes out a headlamp, which she straps on.

A satisfied look on her face, Emily stands and begins making her way across the bridge. Once on flat ground, she climbs a few feet into the ravine and pulls Tasha's bike and purple helmet from behind a bush.

I talk to Levi on the way home, trying to get straight what I just saw. "Jennifer, Alyssa, and Danielle can't stand Emily. Plus, Jennifer somehow thinks Emily's interested in Michael. They decide to prank her. At night, all four of them ride their bikes to the bridge area. The girls hide Emily's bike and pretend to ride off. Emily goes out on the bridge and won't get off even when they return with her bike. Jennifer loses it and pushes Emily's bike into the ravine."

Levi stops to pee, and I wait for her.

"Okay, but here's where it gets weird," I say when we start walking again. "Emily pulled out Tasha's bike from behind a bush. Where she must have hidden it earlier, maybe like the day before or something. So Emily knew about the girls' plan. She wasn't ever going to jump to her death. She went out on the bridge and basically started screaming and insulting Jennifer, Alyssa, and Danielle, annoying them on purpose."

I throw the stick, and Levi bounds into the woods to retrieve it.

"The last time those girls saw Emily, she was acting like a total wack job on a bridge. For all they know, she did jump, and they didn't tell anybody. They let the police start their investigation in the wrong place." I throw the stick again.

Levi brings back the stick, and we walk along the highway's soft shoulder.

"You know what?" I say slowly. "Emily set that whole thing up. She wanted Jennifer to shove her bike over the edge. She went out of her way to push Jennifer's buttons." I pause, thinking. "Emily didn't want the girls to know what happened to her."

But why did Emily fake her own disappearance?

And where is she now?

CHAPTER 19

*T*he school attendance clerk calls the next morning while my mom's in the shower. Apparently, there's a problem with the phone-in line, and I've been marked truant for the last two days. I tell her I had the flu and will be at school today.

Between second and third period, Jennifer, Alyssa, and Danielle find me. They circle around me, flapping their arms and fluttering their hands.

Jennifer reaches out and pretends to pluck something from my shoulder.

I'm trapped as they flit about, imitating me. My face grows warm, and my muscles tense.

"Look at me." Jennifer dances by me. "I'm a butterfly. A butterfly thief. A KleptoRainia."

It doesn't even make sense. Jennifer's such a moron.

The other two girls laugh at Jennifer's stupid comments.

Why are teachers and hall monitors never around when you need them?

Alyssa waves her hands close to my face. "What do you think of my sweater, Raine? Like it? Gonna steal it?" she says in a singsong voice.

"How about my phone?" Jennifer joins in. "Gonna steal that, too?"

I'm waiting for Danielle to take a turn when suddenly the fire alarm goes off, a loud, nonstop ringing.

The hall immediately fills with students swarming toward the exits.

"See you later, girlfriend," Jennifer says with a sickly sweet smile.

Alyssa and Danielle wave.

Then I'm swept along with the crowd and out through the double doors. The front lawn is jammed with students and teachers. My fingers are tingling as if I stuck them wet into an electrical outlet. There must be scads of sparkles around, but I'm only seeing a few. I shove my hands deep in my jean pockets.

Outside, Torie, Willow, Sydney, and a few other cross-country runners call me over to where they're standing by the flagpole.

"You okay?" Willow asks, examining my face.

"I'm fine." There's no point describing the whole dancing circle of embarrassment. I'll be dealing with those girls for a while, a long while. I sigh.

"One of the equipment sheds is totally in flames," Torie says excitedly. "Started with black smoke, but now, wow."

"Which shed?" Willow asks.

"The one next to the—"

The whine of a fire truck siren cuts Torie off. Lights flashing, the truck speeds past the main entrance and turns into the drive that leads to the back of the school and the track.

"Tennis courts," Torie finishes.

"Do you think it was set on purpose?" Willow asks. "We've had a lot of fires around Yielding lately."

"My dad says we need real firefighters," another girl chimes in. "The volunteers can't keep up."

Shirlee wanders over and stands next to me. "The sheds are locked at night. I guess this means he started the fire from outside."

"My sister could totally touch that up." Torie grabs my hand with the tattoo and holds it next to hers.

Willow and Sydney stretch out their arms to compare.

"Yours really faded fast," Sydney says to me.

"She'd do it for free," Torie says. "Different skin types process the henna dye differently."

"That's okay," I say, feeling bad that I tried to erase my tattoo and they didn't.

Garrett gets busted by a teacher when he pulls out a small football and starts tossing it back and forth with another guy.

Hugh's standing with a knot of friends, Avalon draped over his shoulder like a rash. Suddenly he steps back and bursts out laughing. He's laughing so hard, Avalon unwinds herself from him and stands forlornly on her own. Someone else in the group adds a comment, and Hugh laughs again, shaking his head. When he stops laughing and steps back into the group, Avalon rearranges herself on his arm.

The buzzer sounds to signal the return to class. Mr. Gates walks beside me. "Why would anyone burn down our equipment shed?"

"Do you think it's the same person who's been lighting fires in the woods around town?" I ask. I pluck a sparkle off the grade book he's carrying.

"I have no idea." He shakes his head sadly, then makes a beeline for Garrett, who's hanging at the end of the line, bouncing the plastic football off the backs of unsuspecting students.

The sparkle shows Mr. Gates grading tests. Danielle got a D.

The rest of the morning goes okay. The fire pretty much dominates all of today's conversations, although I definitely notice a few people staring at me. In the hall, a guy I don't know walks next to me, his movements all jerky, like a strobe light's shining on him. His friends laugh. I have no idea what that's about and just ignore him. Luckily, I don't have any more run-ins with Jennifer and her friends. There's an announcement canceling cross-country practice because the fire department's investigating near the track and the locker room, trying to get a handle on how it all went down.

Near the end of lunch, Torie passes by me while I'm throwing out my trash. "Don't stress about the YouTube video of you, Raine. It's barely getting any views."

CHAPTER 20

A YouTube video of me?

This can't be good.

There's about ten minutes left in lunch. I text Shirlee.

Where are you?

Library.

She's in a corner at the back, flipping quickly through a Spanish dictionary. "I forgot this assignment was due today," she grumbles.

"Can I see your phone?" I ask, wishing for the millionth time that I had a smartphone and could be online anytime, anywhere.

She inclines her head toward her backpack. "In the front pocket."

I push open the door to the courtyard and quickly find the video Torie was talking about. Even though I'm alone, my face goes warm at the title. "KleptoRainia." Posted this morning by "Police Watch."

It's a ninety-second clip that starts with a shot of Jennifer's necklace hanging from a hook in a locker. Then it's my head, not attached to my body, turning right, right, right, then left, left, left. Over and over and over. All jerky and animated, checking to see if I'm being watched. Then an arm, not mine, although the viewer is supposed to think it is, reaches out. Over and over and over. At a fast speed, then in slow motion. Then it's the head-turning thing again. Then a hand grabs the necklace, three, four, five, six times. And drops it multiple times into a backpack. The video ends with a shot of my face in a wanted poster.

I wish the crack in the asphalt would widen and suck me down to the molten lava in the middle of the earth.

I check the screen again. Torie's right. There aren't a ton of views, about twenty. So far. Was Hugh one of those twenty views? Obviously the guy in the hall earlier saw it and was mimicking me.

When I slip the phone back in its pocket, Shirlee's scribbling like the Energizer Bunny on caffeine. She's on the last row of words and not even bothering to dot the *i*'s: *la pijama, el bolso, el impermeable.* Her eyes flitting from the dictionary to the paper, she asks if everything's okay.

"Yeah." My voice squeaks. "Thanks."

"Los jeans," she mutters under her breath.

The bell buzzes. "Later," I say.

"Sí," she answers, still writing.

In the afternoon, whether I'm walking down the hall or sitting in class, I feel like I'm getting all sorts of knowing looks. I go around every corner, my throat tight, anxious Jennifer's lying in wait.

With leaden feet, I make my way extra slowly up the stairs to last period, where I know I'll see Jennifer and the others. And Hugh.

A guy from English bumps into me. "Sorry." He goes around me. "Hilarious YouTube, by the way." He gallops off, two stairs at a time.

When I get to film, Mr. Magee's got everyone divided into groups, where they're huddled and working.

"Raine." He points to the far corner.

As I pass Jennifer's group, she and Alyssa imitate the head movement in the video. Of course Mr. Magee is oblivious.

I join Shirlee, Willow, and a girl with a braid.

"We're writing movie reviews," Shirlee explains.

It takes our group forever to get through the list. Partly because Braid Girl's only seen five movies in her whole life. Partly because Shirlee and Willow can't agree on anything.

They bicker like chipmunks, chattering high and fast and gesturing with quick, nervous movements. On a different day, they would actually be funny to watch.

No one mentions YouTube. Maybe they don't know about it. In my brain, it's playing on a repeating loop.

A couple of times, Shirlee taps my shoulder. "Raine?"

"Having a little trouble concentrating," I say.

By the time our group finishes, hands in the work, and gets the okay to leave, the rest of the class is long gone.

"Remember," Mr. Magee says, "tomorrow's the first check-in for your projects. Worth a lot of points. You and your partner should have a very detailed outline."

Are Hugh and I still on for tonight? I swallow. I wonder what he thinks of me and the whole stealing thing. Does he know about the video?

As I'm sliding my binder into my backpack, Mr. Magee walks over. "Everything okay?" he asks in a low voice.

"Yeah," I say, pushing back my chair. Has he seen the video?

When I get home, I text Hugh. No response.

The only person I get a text from is my mom.

Won't be home for dinner. Going out with
people from office. Microwave frozen meal?

And so begins the death of the fresh start. Mom's had lots of late nights. How many for work? How many for fun? My loser boyfriend antennae are waving madly. But instead of the usual dread, I'm filled with a grim satisfaction.

"The Queen of Rebound is going out tonight," I say to Levi, who also knows exactly how this will play out.

"First comes love. Then comes letdown. Then comes packing up the truck and waving goodbye to Yielding," I chant.

Close to six-thirty, I walk over to the Jitter Bean.

I tell my stomach to smarten up and untangle itself. Hugh's either there or he's not. He thinks I'm a thief or he doesn't. He's seen the video or he hasn't. But stressing won't change things. Too bad stomachs are bad listeners.

The bell tinkles as I push open the door. The coffee shop isn't empty, but it isn't overly crowded. I easily scan the place. Hugh isn't here.

But Avalon is. She's camped out in the corner, surrounded by books. Her head's down; she's totally focused on whatever she's reading. Her face is so close to the page, it looks like she's underlining words with the tip of her nose. It's weird seeing her without Hugh. It's like half her body got amputated. Either she doesn't notice me or she's ignoring me.

A few seventh graders are working at the big table in the quiet room. They barely glance at me, and I don't think I register on their radar. Is my story only eighth-grade news?

It's still a few minutes before six-thirty. I must've walked faster than usual.

I go back to the front and order a mug of hot chocolate from the guy behind the counter.

At a table on the opposite side of the room from Avalon,

141

I turn on my computer. While it's booting up, I check my phone. No text from Hugh. No missed call.

I log on to the coffee shop's Internet and go straight to YouTube. Up to fifty views. Two are mine. I do not need this thing to go viral.

Scraping off little spoonfuls of whipped cream, I eat slowly and read over my project notes. I stretch out the hot chocolate, drinking it in baby sips.

Still no Hugh.

After fifteen or so minutes, I text him. Why not? If he's not coming, he should at least have the decency to let me know. Still, I have a sinking feeling.

A half hour ticks by. The seventh graders file past. My mug is bone-dry. I've memorized my notes, along with every crack and scratch on the table. The sinking feeling has morphed into a drowning feeling.

The bell on the door rings. Both Avalon and I look up.

It's not Hugh.

A girl from my Spanish and film classes marches in.

"Celine," Avalon says. "Over here."

Celine smiles. She pulls out a chair at Avalon's table and hangs a computer bag over the back. "You get much done?" she asks.

"Kinda." Avalon waves a hand over the papers on the table. "I don't know if you'll like it, though."

"I'll show you what I got." Celine pulls a laptop from the bag and turns it on. "Magee's gonna love it."

Apparently, they're meeting for their film project, too.

The bell on the door tinkles again.

It's Hugh. "Hey, Avalon, Celine." He turns to me. "Sorry, Raine. I got here as fast as I could."

An hour late's the best he could do? That's disturbing.

Then, hands in his pockets, he saunters over to Avalon and pretends to read her papers. "We might be able to use some of these ideas in our project," he calls across the room to me.

Avalon giggles.

"Get lost, Hugh," Celine says.

"We'll just be over there"—he jerks a head in my direction—"if you two need any help."

"No thanks." Celine rolls her eyes. "We want a good grade."

Avalon giggles again. She has an irritating giggle, like her nose is partially plugged.

Celine stands. "Come on, Avalon. We're moving to the back room. Where we can work in peace."

Avalon hops right up. Apparently, she's used to being bossed around by Celine.

Hugh walks over to me. He shrugs off his backpack and sits. "You want a doughnut or anything? Remember, it's on the house."

"I kind of just want to get started." I sound annoyed.

Hugh frowns. "Avalon told you what happened, right? And that I'd be late."

"No," I say flatly.

Hugh shakes his head. "She's not always reliable."

Yes, she is, I think. *Reliably mean.*

"Buttons ate my cell phone."

"You're kidding." Is there even room inside Buttons for a phone?

"I bet Levi's never given you a scare like that."

"Nope," I say. "So how's Buttons doing?"

"The vet said he'll be okay."

"How'd you figure it out?"

"I didn't. Buttons started vomiting all over the place about an hour after I got home from school. The vet did an X-ray. My phone was in his stomach, next to a golf tee and a quarter."

"I can't believe it."

"The vet said if we didn't do surgery, Buttons would die. That's where I was till now. The surgery just ended."

"Did he learn a lesson? Or will he just keep on eating stuff?"

"He starts 'consumption therapy' next week." Hugh pulls a notebook and a pen from his backpack.

"I've never even heard of consumption therapy."

"Be glad."

We get going on our project. Both of us did some work ahead of time, and we just trade ideas and take some of mine and some of his. For the first time all day, I relax. I'm in a bubble where all the ugliness of the previous hours can't get in. I stretch out my legs and cross them, at ease.

About an hour in, Hugh's trying to convince me that videotaping at the dump is a stellar idea.

"But we're showing a day in the life of a Yielding Middle School student," I say. "Who goes to the dump? No one."

"True." Hugh tips back his chair and laces his hands behind his head. "But the dump is part of Yielding, and I bet no one else will film there. So we'll get extra points for originality. And I could use the extra points."

"No one else will film there because it doesn't make sense," I argue.

"You gotta think outside the box." Hugh draws a square in the air and points at it. "Box." He points away from it. "Extra points."

Avalon beckons from the back of the room. "Time for a break, Hugh. Celine and I are watching some cool stuff on YouTube." Her smile is sly, and her eyes slide past me.

Pop. So much for the safe bubble.

Hugh stands. "Coming?" he asks me.

I shake my head. I'd rather eat glass. The second Hugh turns the corner to the back room, I start packing up. I can't see any way this scenario is going to end okay.

When I swing my backpack over my shoulder, it knocks my empty hot chocolate mug to the ground. Where it shatters into a million pieces. Deafeningly.

Everyone in the room looks up.

I freeze. Little shards of ceramic glitter on the floor. Some right by my feet. Some have skidded under a nearby table. What am I supposed to do?

"Just give me a sec," says the guy at the front counter.

Of course he's in the middle of serving someone, so I'm

basically stuck, standing in a puddle of broken mug, not sure if I should stay to clean up my mess. Really, I just want to run out the door.

The guy holds up his index finger, signaling that he'll be there in one minute. He disappears down the hall.

Suddenly Hugh's walking toward me. He glances at the table, at the backpack over my shoulder, and at the broken mug on the floor.

"Quick," he says. "Let's split before I get stuck sweeping up."

"I've been thinking it over," he says once we're in the parking lot.

I go cold. What? What's he been thinking over? He doesn't want to be my partner?

"You're right about the dump. It doesn't fit. So I'm willing to deal on that, but you gotta deal on which restaurant we shoot a scene at."

"I can do that," I say.

He walks me home without mentioning the YouTube video.

And for the first time ever, I understand why my mother falls hard for guys. Because I can feel myself starting to fall for Hugh and his messy hair and crazy jokes and knack for knowing what not to talk about.

CHAPTER 21

$\mathcal{T}$he next week and a half stretches out and feels like a horrible forever. "Hey, KleptoRainia," Jennifer always starts with. Her voice is friendly, her smile big. It's an act. Her eyes are cruel and icy cold. But teachers and hall monitors don't notice.

So when Jennifer, Alyssa, and Danielle surround me and hem me in daily, often more, everyone walks by. No one stops them.

Jennifer uploads a few more videos on YouTube about me, then stops. It's not really her thing. She prefers to bully in real life, up close and personal. She wants to see her victim's reaction.

The first couple of days I talked back in the circle, tried

to push my way out. Until I saw how that made Jennifer's eyes light up, made her smile with triumph. So I stopped reacting. I want her to get bored with tormenting me.

When my mom asks me about school, I tell her it's all fine. There's nothing she can do. And talking about it would only make it worse. Anyway, she's staying out late more and more. I don't ask questions, don't nag, don't try to nudge her back onto the fresh-start track. At this rate, we'll be out of Yielding way before the end of eighth grade. That idea keeps me sane.

That and running. All my frustration pours out at practice. I'm getting faster and stronger. The coach moved me up to varsity. I'll beat Jennifer.

This morning, Jennifer, Alyssa, and Danielle crowd in tight, poking me.

"How're you today?" Jennifer elbows me in the side. "Find anything to steal?"

Inside the circle, it's close and warm. There's a nauseating smell of deodorants and perfumes. Danielle has bacon breath. When Jennifer shakes her head, swinging her necklace, it's almost like Emily is stuck in here with me.

"Why isn't she doing our homework?" Danielle asks.

"Duh," Jennifer laughs. "We don't want our grades to go down."

One of the girls pinches the back of my arm. Hard. And then, suddenly, they stop and take off down the hall. Until the next time.

If someone were taking photos, I'd show up as a shadow.

Gray and flimsy. Muted. It's how I deal with Jennifer. If there were a gifted class for cruelty, she'd be in it.

After lunch, I get my afternoon books from my locker. Walking down the hall, I keep an eye out for Jennifer. If I can avoid her by taking a different route, I do. I could be a tour guide for Yielding Middle. I know every nook and cranny of the place.

Instead, I see Shirlee. She's standing outside a restroom door. She's hunched over and as pale as if she crawled out from inside a coffin. Her hair is limp, and her bottom lip trembles. The word to describe Shirlee is *traumatized*. She is traumatized at the thought of pushing open the restroom door. Jennifer has traumatized her.

"Hey, Shirlee," I say softly.

She jumps, her hand clutching her chest.

"Hi." Her voice is low, barely above a whisper. She shuffles a little closer to the door, then stops and stares, gnawing on her lip. "Could you help me?" she finally asks.

"What do you need me to do?" I'm already dreading the answer because I'm realizing that a shadow doesn't have a lot of courage. That turning myself into a shadow isn't outwitting Jennifer. It's making me less of a person.

"Could you make sure Jennifer's not in the bathroom?" She looks at me beseechingly, like one of those poor, dressed-in-rags kids on TV who are begging with a tin cup.

I place my palm flat against the door and begin to push. The door inches open. I hear echoey voices. My hand flies off the door like it's on fire. I don't know who's in there. But it could be Jennifer.

"I never know where she is." Shirlee blinks back tears. "You know when the weather's dry and you get static electric shocks off almost everything you touch? Then it gets to the point that you're scared to touch anything? I'm scared of everything."

This picture is seriously wrong. Shirlee and I are cowering in front of a door. We're nervous and shaky each time we step into the hall. Shirlee wants to go back to homeschooling. I want to move. All because of one girl. One mean, conniving girl who wakes up every morning determined to make our lives a little more miserable.

Something in me snaps. I clear my throat. I shake my head. I straighten my shoulders. I'm Superman throwing open the phone-booth door, waving his cape. I'm a butterfly busting out of a cocoon. I'm an eighth grader who's done with being bullied.

"I have an idea." I take her hand and lead her to the nurse's office. "She got her period early," I say to the nurse when we arrive.

"Supplies are in the bathroom." The nurse looks up from her desk where she's filling out paperwork.

When Shirlee's finished, I take her hand again. We walk through the hall, past the office, and out the front door.

"Where are we going?" she asks.

"To Grinders," I say. "Where we can plan in peace with

a hot chocolate." I look her in the eye, holding her gaze. "It has to stop. We have to stop her. And I have an idea."

Bert's behind the counter. Does he ever go home? Or can he add "haven't left Grinders in forty years" to his resume, too?

He nods at us, and the sunlight streaming through the window bounces halo-like off his bald head. "Lunch, ladies?"

I start to say no because I don't have money, when Shirlee interrupts me. "Sure. Two specials." She squeezes my arm. "My treat."

"Thanks," I say.

There's a noisy card game going on at one table, and a quiet game of cribbage between two white-haired ladies at another. Another table's discussing the latest fire. Apparently, a shed burned down at Yielding Elementary last night. A few people sit alone with a newspaper. Everyone has a beige plate with a croissant sandwich, ruffled potato chips, and a dill pickle.

Shirlee and I sit opposite each other at "our" booth.

Before my eyes, Shirlee transforms back into her normal self. Her face pinks up. Her eyes sparkle. Her lips curve up in a smile. "Want to hear your latest horoscope?"

"Sure." I lean back, stretching out my legs. "Does it have anything to do with courage?"

"More like"—she slaps a hand over her heart—"romance."

I groan. "No, no. I want courage, cunning, and karma."

"Oops." Shirlee shrugs. "Instead you get 'Romance is just around the corner.' I can email you the rest of the details when I get home, if you want."

"No, it's okay."

"Maybe Hugh?" She opens her eyes wide.

"I don't think so," I say. "Let me explain to you in three syllables why that won't work: *Av-a-lon.*"

Shirlee doesn't look convinced.

Bert arrives with our lunch specials: the same beige plates with the same meal as the rest of the coffee shop.

I must look surprised, because both Bert and Shirlee laugh.

"We only serve one lunch," Bert says. "I change up the meat every few days, depending on what's on sale." He leaves us and goes to peer over the shoulders of the card players.

Shirlee bites in and chews. "You have some sort of plan?" she asks after swallowing.

"Remember that time in the bathroom when I mentioned a guy named Michael who wasn't into Jennifer? Remember how she totally shut up?"

Shirlee sucks in her cheeks, like I pulled a plug on her head.

"What if we make her believe Michael likes her? Really likes her. And then he humiliates her."

Shirlee wrinkles her forehead. "How?"

"I have contact info for everyone on the cross-country team. Which means I have Jennifer's cell number. You have a phone with a number she won't recognize." I pick up a chip. "We'll text her, pretending to be Michael."

"What happens when he texts her for real?" Shirlee asks.

"Trust me. He's never texting her." I nibble. "Never."

"You said before that taking down the mean girl could go really, really wrong," Shirlee says slowly.

"We were afraid to push open a bathroom door." I pause to let our pitifulness sink in. "How much more wrong could it go?" Of course I don't mention Emily Huvar. I don't know how wrong it went for her.

Shirlee closes her eyes, thinking. Then she opens them and hands me her phone.

It's a fairly new phone, thin and light with a cool protective gel case. I'm having smartphone envy. I'm probably the only eighth grader in Yielding without a smartphone. But we can't afford the monthly data charges.

I jiggle my foot, mulling over a few possibilities, then type.

Hi. Its Michael. Got new phone. Wanted to give u my number. Sup?

CHAPTER 22

$\mathcal{I}$'m walking up the driveway when Mrs. Burns's side door swings open.

She marches across the yard, a determined look on her face. "You're playing hooky!" she barks.

She's right. I'm ditching school and practice. I scratch my back through my T-shirt. "I have a very contagious rash."

She raises her drawn-on eyebrows. "I know exactly how you got that rash."

Did not see that coming. "You do?"

"Roaming the neighborhood during the wee hours. I saw you last night, all dressed in black, sneaking into your house at two in the morning. Again."

Did not see that coming, either.

She starts blasting away about underhanded, dishonest teens. I dial her down until all I hear is "blah, blah, blah," which is good background noise while I contemplate what she said.

Who could Mrs. Burns be mistaking me for? Not Tasha. She's too short. It must've been my mother. We're close to the same height and build. And my mom does wear a lot of dark colors, because apparently they're slimming.

My mother went to the movies with her work buddies last night. Did she end up staying out till two in the morning with a loser?

Mrs. Burns notches up her pitch and is lecturing me on not ending up like Emily.

I interrupt. "*Again?* You said *again*?"

"I lost track after twelve. Probably more. Sometimes you're sneaking in. Sometimes you're sneaking out. It's not as if I'm standing guard by the window."

More likely she's standing guard by the window with binoculars. "Twelve?" I'm blown away by the number. How did I not realize this? And how did my mom feel even marginally honest with her this-is-the-last-fresh-start-we're-staying-in-Yielding-and-living-happily-ever-after speech?

"As if you didn't know." She gives me a look people use for cockroaches. "I'll be speaking to your mother, young lady."

I go inside and start my homework. I'm still puzzling over the first math problem when my phone lights up with a text from Shirlee.

She answered.

That was fast. Apparently, Jennifer's texting from film.

Forward me her text, I type.

Michael White?????

Tell her yes. I hit send.

Freaking out. Can't do this. You can have my phone and text her. Shirlee's panic comes through with her message.

Ok.

In minutes, there's machine-gun banging at my door. Shirlee's breathing hard. Her face is shiny. Her backpack's half hanging off her shoulder. She must've made a quick U-turn before even getting home. "Here." Her phone dangles from between her thumb and index finger like she's afraid it's got malaria or something.

I look at the messages. "She's been blowing up your phone." I widen the door. "I was doing math homework. Well, more like staring it down. Operation Retaliation will be way more interesting."

Shirlee stares at me like I've totally lost it. "Aren't you nervous?"

"No." And I'm not. I'm energized and empowered. Not to sound too cliché, but I'm doing this for me. For Shirlee. For Emily, wherever she may be.

"There's no guarantee this won't backfire." Shirlee's still staring, like maybe she can stare some sense into me.

"There are no guarantees anywhere in life." I say this from my own experiences and from what I've seen in other people's memories. "Anyway, it's worth the risk."

Shirlee follows me to the kitchen, and we sit next to each other on barstools. Levi pads down the hall and lies on the rug in front of the sink.

"Okay, Jennifer. What have you been saying?" I press the messages button.

Michael White?????

When there was no response, Jennifer sent another text.

Is it really you?

And when there was no response again, she sent another text.

My girlfriends don't think I should text you back.

I type. Yes. It's me. Sorry. Couldn't text. Why don't your friends want you to text me?

"You approve?" I ask Shirlee.
"I guess." But she shakes her head.

Bec you were horrible to me, Jennifer sends.

I wasn't that horrible.

U were 2.

What if I apologize? I smile.

"You're flirting with her." Shirlee is shocked.

That might help, Jennifer messages.

Ltr. Gotta go.

"When is 'later'?" Shirlee asks.

"When we feel like it," I say, shrugging. "Seriously, I don't know. What do you think?"

"Tomorrow? Let her check her phone every five minutes in the meantime."

"Sounds good to me."

We do homework together for a couple of hours. Shirlee helps me with math. It'll be the first time in years I show all the work and get all the answers right. Score.

When Shirlee's phone buzzes, we both jump. But it's just her mom, telling her to come home for dinner.

"I guess nothing will change tomorrow," she says wistfully, closing her science book.

"With Jennifer? No, not that fast. But it'll change at some point. Thanks to Operation Retaliation." I roll out the words.

She slides her phone in her pocket and picks up her backpack by the loop.

At the front door, her phone buzzes again. She pulls it out. "Jennifer." There's excitement in her voice. She reads aloud, "Sup?"

"She's impatient," I say. "That'll help us."

"You want to respond?"

"No," I say. "Let's go with your plan."

After Shirlee leaves, I take Levi for a walk, feed her, then do more homework.

I'm in the middle of atoms and molecules when the key turns in the porch door. "Raine?" my mom calls. "Did you see the side of the house?"

"Why?" I meet her at the door.

"Just something that will make you happy," my mom replies cryptically.

We peer around the porch. Leaning against the wall is a mattress. Next to it are several flattened cardboard boxes.

"I cleaned out the basement yesterday," she says when I don't jump up and down with joy. "And replaced the lightbulb because there wasn't one. Guess what I found? Washer and dryer hookups."

"No," I say firmly. "I will never go into a basement to do laundry. My clothes could be so stiff with dirt, they walk to school on their own, and I still wouldn't do it."

My mother laughs. "I'd go down and do the laundry. You could fold in the living room." She sighs. "I'm so tired of Laundromats."

I scan her for sparkles, hoping for a heads-up on last night. Nothing. "Mrs. Burns was over earlier," I say. "Where were you last night?"

"The movies," she says.

"What's his name?"

I can tell from the way her shoulders hitch up that she's drawing in a deep, calming breath. "Derek."

I feel like I took one to the stomach. Derek. The name makes it real. "What's all this?" I make a sweeping motion toward the mattress and broken-down boxes. "What's all the fresh-start crapola about?"

"I'm not getting involved with him. The secretary at work arranged for him to come out with us last night. I didn't even know about the setup."

"You were out till two in the morning."

My mother wrinkles up her face in puzzlement. "What?"

"Mrs. Burns said she saw someone sneaking back into our house at two in the morning. Who else would it be?"

"She must've been confused. I was home by midnight. Maybe she woke up in the middle of the night and was still half-asleep. Who knows what she saw. A dog? A cat? A tree?"

"Was she confused twelve times?" My hands are on my hips.

"What do you mean?"

"She said she saw someone sneak in or out at least twelve different times."

"Don't you think you'd notice if I was out that much?" my mom says reasonably. "Twelve is a lot. I've only been out a few times. Four, tops."

I nod. I definitely would've noticed twelve times. Mrs. Burns must be losing it. She's old.

"I really am trying," Mom says.

I believe her. I believe she's really trying to make it work in Yielding. The problem is that trying and succeeding can be hundreds of miles apart.

That's why I wait till she goes to bed before rummaging through the kitchen trash for a movie ticket stub.

CHAPTER 23

*M*y mother is not a liar. At least, not on purpose. If she said she was going to the movies with a group from work, she did. If she said she told Derek she wasn't in the dating game, she did. It's the between-the-lines stuff I worry about. The "meta message," as Mr. Magee says.

I need a sparkle. A sparkle with a memory about last night. I could watch my mom in action and judge for myself. Not that I seem to have any control over when sparkles and memories show up. But I have to try.

I stamp on the kitchen trash can pedal, popping up the lid. My fingers immediately begin to tingle. There, lounging at the top of the contents, is half a Yielding Cinemas ticket. No sparkle, but the tingling fingers give me hope.

I set the ticket in my palm and stare at it till my eyes go blurry. Nothing. I hold the ticket tight and close my eyes. Still nothing. On the counter, I place the same candle I used to pull the memory from Jennifer's necklace. I listen to the same tracks on my laptop. Nothing. Nothing. Nothing. What's the deal? If it weren't for my fingers, I'd swear the ticket didn't have a sparkle.

Finally, beyond frustrated, I give up. I'll have to trust my mother. Trust. That's a novel concept when it comes to my mother and relationships.

I drop the torn ticket back in the trash, giving the can an annoyed kick.

That's when I notice a little sparkle fighting its way up from beneath some broken eggshells and a wet tea bag. I poke these things aside, clearing a path. The little sparkle shines brighter now, its points white-hot, jumping toward me from a crumpled Uncle Bob's Peanut Butter Protein Bar wrapper.

Some runners have lucky socks. Some have lucky shoes. I have my lucky Uncle Bob's Peanut Butter Protein Bars. I got hooked on them when we lived in Tennessee, three moves ago. Now my mom orders them from a store in Nashville, and when you add up shipping and the cost of the bars, they're pricey. I eat one, and only one, the morning of race day. For every record I've set, every event I've won, there's been an Uncle Bob's Peanut Butter Protein Bar in my stomach.

I brought my remaining three bars from Detroit and

stored them at the back of the kitchen cupboard, keeping them safe until the first invite. My mom's deathly allergic to peanuts. She wouldn't go near an Uncle Bob's Peanut Butter Protein Bar, never mind unwrap one.

Who ate my bar and dumped the wrapper in our trash? Has Tasha been back? Did I misjudge her, and she actually does have another spare key?

Whose memory is flashing at me?

I reach for the wrapper. I fold my fingers over my palm and close my eyes.

They fly back open.

It can't be!

I tighten my grip and close my eyes again.

Muttering under her breath, Emily Huvar is rooting around in our kitchen cupboard. In one hand, she holds a small flashlight. In the other, she's grasping an Uncle Bob's Peanut Butter Protein Bar.

Suddenly she freezes, a look of panic on her face. She switches off the flashlight and drops to her knees at the far end of the counter.

Rubbing my eyes, I stumble to the sink and fill a glass with water. I reach up to close the cupboard Emily left ajar. I sip water, then, yawning, shuffle out of the kitchen, inches from where Emily's hiding. There's a creak when I step on the middle of the third stair leading to my bedroom.

Still crouching, her head tilted, Emily listens and waits. After several minutes, she stands and tiptoes through the

kitchen, very slowly opens the door leading to the basement,
then heads downstairs, the flashlight beam bouncing off the
concrete steps.

In the corner of the room, she plunks down on a mat-
tress covered with a sleeping bag. She unwraps the protein bar
halfway and begins eating. She sits quietly for a few minutes,
enjoying the bar, then stands, pulls on a dark hoodie, and
swings a black backpack over her shoulder.

She tiptoes upstairs. Back in the kitchen, she clamps the
remaining part of the bar between her front teeth and shines
the flashlight into the cupboard. With her free hand, she
pushes the protein bar box with its sunshine-yellow letters
and cartoon picture of Uncle Bob to the back of the cupboard.
She pauses, then sticks her hand in the box and snags another
bar, which she shoves in her pocket.

She crumples the wrapper of the bar she's eating and drops
it in the trash.

Emily Huvar is living in our basement.

And I almost met her one night when I got up for a
drink of water.

Levi must be so used to her that she doesn't even consider Emily an intruder.

It's as if I'm in my running zone. Every thought in my
head is crystal clear.

Emily Huvar is alive. And living in our basement. She
convinced Jennifer and the others to abandon her at the
bridge, then stayed hidden in Yielding.

I wander through the kitchen to the living room to the bathrooms to the bedrooms. The entire house looks different, feels different. I've crossed over to another world. A world where missing girls hide out in basements.

It certainly explains a lot. Like the weird creaking and groaning sounds that wake me up at night. That's Emily moving around the house, opening and closing cupboards and doors. Like Tasha showing up with a grocery bag full of sandwiches and a magazine Emily used to read. She must visit often to drop off supplies for her sister. Like the neighbor thinking she saw me sneaking back into our house late at night, when she actually spotted Emily.

I come to an abrupt stop.

Why? Why did Emily fake her own disappearance?

And then several more questions tumble into my head. Has she been living in our house since her family was evicted? Where was she before then? Besides Tasha, and now me, does anyone else know? Her parents? Where does Emily go late at night?

One person can answer all those questions.

Emily and I need to meet.

I press my ear against the door to the basement. Silence.

I can't go down there. I can't. Beads of sweat collect under my arms. I shake from the legs of imaginary spiders crawling all over me.

I slide down the wall and sit, my back against the frame.

Levi lies next to me, her head at my thigh and her tail at my feet. Emily will trip over us if she tries to go out tonight.

Weird how the only memory I picked up of Emily was her lying on the living room carpet, listening to music and reading a magazine. True, I generally don't grab sparkles I see at home, because they're usually boring, everyday memories left behind by my mother or me. But it's not like my fingers are tingling overtime or the house is lit up like the Fourth of July with a bunch of extra sparkles. Maybe Emily mostly stays in the basement. Maybe she only recently started raiding our cupboards because her sister hasn't been dropping off food as often. Since I took her key.

After an hour, I am cold and stiff. I get a thick blanket and pillows and make a bed. I lie there in the dark, wondering what to say to Emily when she goes to step over me. "Hi. I'm Raine." "Do your parents know you're okay?" "Are you completely insane?"

At midnight, Shirlee messages me.

She's texting him.

Saying what? I type.

Watcha doin?

You want to answer? I ask.

Idk. I kinda think he can't keep ignoring her. But I don't know what to say.

Trying to sleep, I suggest.

Ok. Thx.

Shirlee texts again in a few minutes.

Jennifer texted, Sorry. Gd nite. So I texted, Gd nite babe.

Babe? Shirlee's really getting into this.

CHAPTER 24

*T*he morning begins with Levi, me, and a closed door. Emily never left the basement. If she had even cracked the door, I would've woken up.

What now? I think as I walk to school. *Am I going to sleep at the top of the basement stairs every night till Emily comes out? How often does she leave the house?*

Jennifer, Alyssa, and Danielle are lying in wait for me inside the double doors.

"Hi, KleptoRainia," Jennifer says, as usual. That girl is seriously lacking in imagination.

The girls surround me.

"You really like this necklace, don't you?" Jennifer says.

And the stupid comments begin. They're easier to ignore

today. Instead of listening, I watch texts scroll through my head. *Bec you were horrible to me. Watcha doin? Gd nite babe.*

The bell rings, and suddenly it's over. The three of them split up and leave me standing, a new bruise on my calf where someone kicked me.

I'm going from math to history when there's a tap on my shoulder.

"She already texted three times," Shirlee whispers.

"Did you answer?"

"No. You got a second?"

We duck into the library, and Shirlee hands me her phone.

Gd morning! was sent at seven.

??? was sent at eight.

My girlfriends say u wont text me anymore.
came in a few minutes ago.

"Can I take this one?" I say to Shirlee.

"Sure."

Hey babe. Ur girlfriends r idiots. I tilt the screen toward Shirlee.

She frowns.

"It's good. I promise." I press send and give Shirlee her phone.

The bell buzzes, and we hustle to our next class.

The rest of the morning passes uneventfully. Although Señor Lopez decides to spring a pop quiz on us because half the class didn't do last night's homework. And Mrs. Fisher is offering extra credit in history to anyone who dresses up in a Colonial costume, which just sounds lame.

"We were talking about the West Hills Invite," Torie says when I sit down at lunch.

"What about it?" I ask.

"You are so going to place," Sydney says. "And that means a gift certificate. What will you use it for?"

"I haven't won yet." I unwrap my ham sandwich.

Willow doesn't say anything. She doesn't feel great about still being on JV.

Hugh stops at our table.

Avalon and Celine are on the other side of the cafeteria, asking people questions and videoing them.

"I'm picking the restaurant, right?" he says to me. "That's the agreement."

"Not exactly. I said I was willing to compromise."

Like sunflowers turning toward the sun, everyone at the table suddenly tunes in to our conversation.

"Our video for film class," I explain.

"Don't give them any details," Hugh says, "or we'll have to kill them."

I roll my eyes, and that's when I see Jennifer, Alyssa, and Danielle walking toward me. My heart sinks. Not now. Not in front of Hugh. They already got me today.

"Hi, Kle—" Jennifer feels in her pocket. "I got a text," she says to Alyssa and Danielle.

"What's it say?" Alyssa asks.

"High school guy," Jennifer brags to the table at large.

"Can I talk to you privately?" Hugh asks. "I do not want them"—he mock-glares at the girls I'm sitting with—"to hear my plan. They'll steal it."

"We don't need your dumb plan," Torie says. "We have our own."

"Except our plan isn't dumb," Sydney says.

Hugh and I walk to the front of the cafeteria. "I would've texted, but I don't have a new phone."

"How's Buttons?"

"Fine, but I don't think he learned his lesson," Hugh says. "He already went after my pen."

"Maybe he'll improve with therapy."

"Here's hoping." Hugh crosses his fingers. "About the restaurant. I'm thinking Mario's. You make your own pizza."

"Okay."

"My brother can drive us next Thursday. Wanna go right from practice?"

Three syllables, I remind myself. *Av-a-lon. It's not a date. Av-a-lon.* "Sure."

"And he's lending us his hi-res camera," he says.

"Very cool."

"Hugh," Garrett calls from a table of guys. He holds up a milk carton. "I drank your chocolate milk."

"I should have a phone tomorrow." Hugh starts fast-walking toward Garrett. "I gotta save whatever lunch I have left."

Shirlee waits till Hugh leaves before approaching me. She nods at him walking away. "Romance?"

"It's not like that," I say. Although, it is confusing. Because it kind of feels like we're flirting. A little. But there is Avalon. The problem is I don't have tons of experience with guys. "Thanks for saving me with the last text."

She smiles. "I just asked her if she'd gotten the previous message." Shirley hands me the phone to read Jennifer's reply.

My girlfriends r not idiots. That's not nice, Jennifer wrote.

"Because she can recognize nice?" I say sarcastically.

Shirlee smiles. "What next?" She shakes her phone.

"I'm not sure," I say. "Maybe Michael doesn't text anymore today. And we can think about exactly where we're taking this."

Shirlee pushes her phone into my hand. "You're on for tonight."

CHAPTER 25

*W*hen I get home after practice, I tiptoe into the house carefully, shushing Levi. I go straight to the basement door and listen. It's quiet. Is Emily sleeping? Just being super quiet? Is she on the other side, listening? That's a creepy thought.

I slowly turn the knob, then gently push. I peek my head through the doorway. I'm not descending into the spider pit, only looking from the safety of the landing.

It's dusk, and dull gray light filters through small windows that are at ground level. There's a musty, damp smell. I squint. My heart's thudding so hard, I almost expect to see it jump out of my mouth.

I pat the wall for the light switch. Flip. The room is illuminated. The steps down are concrete, but the floor is covered with white linoleum squares that reflect the light from the naked bulb hanging from the ceiling. I like the bright white floor. Spiders can't hide on it.

I go down a step. A single step. I peer around. It's one big room with a furnace in the far corner near the laundry hookups my mom mentioned. Next to the hookups is another door, partly open. A bathroom?

I go down a second step. My hands are clammy.

"Emily," I call softly. "Emily."

Levi whines from the top of the stairs.

"It's okay, Levi. Come on."

She bounds past me and sniffs around the room, tail wagging.

I take a deep breath and walk down the remaining steps. I scour the floor and corners, looking for spiders, my heart beating in my ears. There's a web up high, across the room from me. I bite my lip. Not going there. I peek through the doorway by the furnace. It's a tiny bathroom, with a rusty toilet and a small pedestal sink. The faucet drips.

There's no furniture, no clothing, no towel, no nothing. No sign of anyone. It feels empty.

"Emily," I call more loudly, and my voice echoes.

Not to be dramatic, but it's like I'm in an old black-and-white horror movie, waiting for the bad guy with a knife to lunge out.

My fingers tingle. So there are memories around, but they could be from anyone, anytime. I'm not seeing sparkles. And I'm definitely not hanging down here long enough to check out the whole room, hoping to find them. A spider could land on my head at any moment.

And then I see it.

Behind the furnace. It's the magazine that fell out of Tasha's grocery bag. She must've returned a different time to give it to her sister.

I bend down to pick it up.

A hairy spider, the size of my fist, crawls down the wall and straight toward me.

I scream and race up the stairs. Levi follows. I slam the door.

I am never going down there again. Mom can forget about hooking up a washer and dryer. I'm never folding, wearing, or even touching clothes that were in a basement that can grow a spider that big.

It takes a while of lying flat on my bed to get my heart down to a healthy rate and convince my body to quit pouring out sweat.

Emily was in our basement. She was probably sleeping on that mattress. But Mom, full of fresh-start fever and determined to settle in, scared her off. Most likely, Emily started looking around for a new hiding place the first time an empty box came winging down the stairs. And she would've left for good when mom threw out her mattress.

So where is Emily?

Her choices seem fairly limited: another empty house, a shed, the woods.

Tasha must know.

I take a shower, getting rid of any possible spider germs, then set up at the counter in the kitchen to do my homework.

Until Shirlee's phone buzzes from my backpack, I forget I was playing Michael this evening.

Jennifer sent a picture of herself at a desk, her face large and distorted with the caption "Doin homework."

Me too.

How was ur day?

Boring, I type.

Why did u start texting me?

It must've taken a backpack of courage on Jennifer's part to send this. In real life, Michael was crystal clear about how he wanted nothing to do with her.

I had this experience.

???

I was hanging out with a girl in my class. I realized I wished it was u.

I can practically feel Cupid's arrow stab Jennifer's chest when I press send. For a second, I feel bad, tricking Jennifer like this. But then I think of how she treats Shirlee and me.

Wow. Incredible, Jennifer texts.

But sthg is bugging me.

What? She replies at lightning speed.

Idk if I should say. I don't want you to take it the wrong way.

I won't. I promise.

I do part of my science worksheet before answering, letting Jennifer worry for twenty minutes.

I said I promise. Jennifer finally can't take it anymore.

It's your friends.

What???

They're immature, I type.

U rele think so?

Def.

Jennifer doesn't answer.

After my Spanish homework, I pick up the conversation.

Hi babe!

U rele think they're immature?

Yup.

R u basing it on that time in the pkg lot? When they were acting goofy?

I guess. And on stuff u said.

I'm trying to be careful. I have no idea how well Michael even knows Alyssa and Danielle.

But u think I'm ok?

Creepy. Like I'm eavesdropping or reading someone's diary.

Yup. It's the most I can type without gagging.

I call Shirlee on her house phone and read her the texts.

"What are you trying to get her to say?" Shirlee asks.

"I'm not picky," I say. "I'll take any kind of trash talk about Alyssa and Danielle."

"Will she?"

"She's a jerk. So, yeah, I think she will."

"I feel kind of gross about this," Shirlee says.

"Honestly? I do, too. I want to take a hot shower and scrub off my skin. But, even more, I want her to leave us alone. All we need is proof of her dogging her friends."

"And then what?" Shirlee asks.

"Then the mean girl's going down."

CHAPTER 26

*V*arsity practice is canceled the next day because the coach is traveling with the JV team for an invite in Albany. After school, I jog home to drop off my backpack, then head over to Yielding Elementary.

Surrounded by moms and a few older brothers and sisters, I wait outside the school. The bike racks are in plain view, and I'm peering at them, looking for Tasha's turquoise bike . . . in a sea of turquoise because, apparently, this is *the* color of the year. Thank you, Tasha, for attaching red streamers to your handlebars.

Now that I've spotted her bike, I find a quiet place under a tree, slump against the trunk, and people watch. It's like being in a foreign country. I just don't fit in. Yeah, we're all humans, but we're not speaking the same language. It's been a long time since I skipped happily out of a classroom to get grabbed up in a hug and taken home for milk and cookies. After my grandmother's death, I became a permanent member of the after-hours-care club.

Avalon shows up on the other side of the courtyard, hanging out on the fringe of the crowd. She must be picking up a little brother or sister. Earbud cords trail from her ears to her pocket, and her lips move as she sings. She turns in a circle, checking everyone out. I'm too low to the ground to be on her radar.

Suddenly her face practically cracks in half with a huge smile. A dark-haired guy walks toward her. When he gets close, she hooks a finger in his belt buckle, pulls him to her, and sticks one of the earbuds in his ear. They stand together, bumping hips, waiting for the bell.

What? Wasn't she glued to Hugh at school today? Maybe she wasn't. Maybe that was yesterday? Or last week? Maybe today she and Celine were interviewing in the cafeteria. Did Hugh and Avalon break up? If you blink, you can miss a middle school romance.

The bell rings, loud and long. The crowd surges forward, including Avalon and Nameless Guy. I stand, scanning the bike racks for Tasha.

There she is. She buckles her helmet, walks her bike to the edge of school property, then climbs on and takes off.

I start a slow run behind her. Way behind her. Tasha would definitely recognize me. So I run, hide behind a streetlight, run, duck under a bush, run, crouch next to a parked car. Very super-spy. I feel ridiculous.

Tasha pulls into a parking lot, carefully winds a chain through her front wheel and the metal stand, then snaps on a lock. She disappears into 7-Eleven and returns with two tall Slurpees, which she balances in the basket hanging from the handlebars.

She takes off again, eventually steering down my street.

Doesn't Tasha know her sister changed camps?

She passes my house and waves to Levi, who's looking out the living room window. Then Tasha veers left at the next street, then right, then right again. She parks her bike at the back of 51 Groveland.

This neighborhood's only a few streets over from mine, but it's several degrees skuzzier. Trash cans squat out by the curb, and the air reeks of baking garbage. Number 51 has a yard of weeds and knee-high grass. The windows are bare and streaked with dirt. I look in. Empty. A door at the back of the house opens and closes, the quick movement mirrored in the front window. Tasha's inside.

I wait across the street, out of sight and in the shadow of an old car. After half an hour, I'm bored and thirsty. So I retrace my steps to the 7-Eleven for a Slurpee, too. I get back into my hiding position by the car. A third of a Slurpee later, Tasha leaves.

I cross the street, walk around to the back, and twist the doorknob. Locked.

I knock.

No one comes to the door.

I knock again. "Emily," I call. "I know you're in there."

No response.

"Emily Huvar, I know you're in there." I emphasize her last name.

The door cracks. "I'm not Emily Huvar. Go away."

I stick my foot in the opening. "Let me in." I pause. "I'm alone."

"No." She hip-pushes the door.

"You have to." I raise my palms. "I know your secret."

The door opens wider. "Hurry," she whispers.

She dashes to the stairs leading to the basement and flies down two at a time.

I freeze on the landing.

"Come down," she says anxiously. "Someone could see you through the windows."

Sunlight illuminates the unfinished basement. Concrete floor, concrete steps, drywall. Two spiderwebs hang in the corners. Two. And that's only at first glance. In other words, this place is an arachnid haven.

I sit on the top step. "I don't do basements."

"One more step? So the door will close?" Her voice shakes. This is what Jennifer does to people. She terrifies them.

I bump down a step and shut the door behind me. It's quiet, just the sounds of our breathing.

With only a few small windows, the basement is bathed

in a dull gray light. My fingers begin to tingle. A sparkle winks at me from a cloth bag lying next to Emily's feet.

Is this really happening? Am I really in a run-down, abandoned house, a few yards from Emily Huvar? *The* Emily Huvar, who disappeared more than three months ago? Who the police couldn't find? Who people thought was kidnapped? And killed?

I'm half afraid to blink in case she disappears again.

"What are you staring at?" Standing in the middle of the room, she frowns at me.

"Sorry, but I just can't believe I found you."

"I can't believe it, either." She definitely sounds annoyed. "Did you tell anyone else?"

"No," I say.

"How did you find me?" she asks. "Tasha?"

"Only sort of. More like a bunch of different things came together." I pause. "I'm Raine, by the way."

"Tasha already told me."

"Do your parents know?" I ask.

"No." She gnaws on a nail.

"Really? Because I think they're worried and sad out of this world."

"You've seen them?" Her voice catches.

"No," I admit. "I'm going by what I read online. And what I can imagine."

Emily sinks to a sleeping bag spread out on the floor. It's the same sleeping bag from the memory when she was eating my protein bar in our basement. Emily's skin hasn't been outside during daylight in weeks and is as pale as the drywall behind her. Her hair is stringy, and the bangs are crooked. Her fingernails are chewed way down.

"How'd you get access to this place?" I ask.

"The previous owners left a spare key under the mat. I'm sure they just forgot about it."

"That was lucky," I say.

"Yeah." Emily rubs her arms, then digs in the cloth bag and pulls out a sweater. "Actually, it was Tasha who found this house on one of her bike rides. I got her to look after your mom started throwing boxes and coming down to the basement."

So I was right. My mother chased Emily off. "Where else have you stayed?"

"For the first few weeks, I was in a vacant cabin in the woods. The cabin was good because the police didn't search out that way. Then my family was evicted from the pink house, where you live, and I moved in there." Emily waves around the room. "This place is the worst. Dirty. Gross. No electricity. No water."

"How much longer are you planning to do this?" I ask.

"Till Saturday." She buttons the sweater. "I hope."

I almost topple off the second step in shock. "Saturday? As in two days from now?"

She nods.

"What's so special about Saturday?"

"The street fair."

I almost topple off again. "You've been in hiding for three-plus months, and you're coming out because of the Yielding street fair? I wasn't even planning to go. It sounds so lame."

She smiles the tiniest of smiles, like she's out of practice. "It's the lamest."

"I don't get it."

Dust swirling around her in the muted sunlight, Emily looks up at me and blinks. "Something big's going to happen during the bonfire."

I wait for her to continue.

She clicks her tongue, thinking. It's how Alyssa described her in the memory in Jennifer's basement.

"The arsonist is setting a shed and a cabin on fire," Emily tells me. "Who knows how many acres of trees will burn, too. The fire department will be busy, monitoring the bonfire in town." She stares at me with huge, dark eyes. "I know who the arsonist is," she says in a chilling, soft voice. "And he knows who I am."

"I thought you disappeared because of Jennifer," I say, confused.

She picks up her Slurpee and plunges the straw up and down to break up the frozen drink. "Last year, at the end of seventh grade, Jennifer got a crush on a sophomore named Michael White. Because I was taking a class at the high school, Jennifer wanted me to get info on him, like if he had a girlfriend or where he lived. We were in the same computer science class, last period. So I followed him home one day. He lives on Sparrow. Number seventy."

I know where Sparrow is. It's on the early-morning cross-country route. Jennifer probably made that happen.

"I told Michael about how Jennifer liked him. He told me to take a hike and to tell Jennifer to take a hike." Emily sips. "Jennifer went ballistic, yelling that it was all my fault, that I didn't try hard enough, that I was trying to wreck her life. The next day, I went back to Michael's house with a letter I'd written about how wonderful Jennifer was." She briefly closes her eyes. "I know how pitiful this all sounds. But it was the only way to get Jennifer off my case. You don't know what she's like, but—"

"I do," I say.

Our eyes meet. Silence. We don't need to talk about how sucky Jennifer makes us feel. We both get it.

"So when I got to Michael's," Emily continues, "the garage door was open. He was hunched over a workbench, his back to me. He went into the house." She shakes her cup. "I ran to the workbench to leave the letter and get out of there before he came back. On the workbench, there were alarm clocks with the backs off: SpongeBob, Mickey Mouse, Minnie Mouse, Shrek, and some Disney princesses. Very creepy. Like a kids' alarm clock graveyard. I heard a toilet flush. I threw the letter onto the workbench, but I missed, and it landed behind the bench. Then I heard footsteps. I took off down the driveway."

I move down a step so as to not miss a word.

"That week, twenty acres burned in the woods east of the highway. On the news, they said a SpongeBob alarm clock sparked the fire. I called the police and told them about Michael." She sighs. "They talked to him. But they weren't convinced he was involved." She gazes at me, her eyes even wider. "But he knew I'd ratted him out."

She stops and swallows. "And he told me the next time I called the cops, he'd take Tasha. He'd take her out to the woods. And he'd burn her bit by bit. Until finally she died."

I stop breathing.

"And the next day, he talked her into getting in his car."

Still not breathing. Getting dizzy.

"He dropped her off in front of my school. To show me he was serious."

I finally suck in some air.

"That's why I disappeared. As long as he thinks I'm dead, Tasha's safe." Her eyes darken till they're black as night. "The next time I go to the police, I'll take evidence to lock him away forever."

"Why'd she get in his car?" I ask.

"Because she thinks everyone's her friend. And because . . ." Emily flaps a hand to say *Whatever*.

Because Tasha's not all there, I think.

"The next week, Michael showed up at school and went around asking students about me. Just to let me know he was checking on me. Jennifer thought I really hadn't pumped her up to him, that I'd trash-talked her instead. Because I wanted him for myself." Emily grimaces. "Danielle told me about the girls' plan to leave me in the woods.

I think she felt bad. And Jennifer's not always nice to her." Emily takes a long drink. "I already knew I had to somehow disappear. So I came up with my own plan that piggybacked on Jennifer's."

I jump. My phone's buzzing in my pocket.

"You're phone's been constantly going off," Emily says. "I'm surprised you didn't notice."

I've missed several calls and texts from Shirlee. I scroll down to the last message.

Help!

CHAPTER 27

$\mathscr{I}$ scan the messages. Jennifer's getting impatient and wants to get together with Michael. Shirlee's freaking out about the whole texting scam.

Hang in there. I'll call in a sec, I message Shirlee.

I look up from my phone to see Emily watching me. She's shivering. How does she deal with the cold at night? Where does she pee? And even if you're a little insane and don't have a spider phobia, this basement makes ours look like a four-star hotel.

"You want to move back to my house?" I ask.

"What about your mother?"

"She's finished with the basement," I say.

"Uh, then, yes, uh, thanks," she says awkwardly, like she's not used to getting gifts from people.

"We should tell her what's going on," I say, the words surprising even me. But sometimes it's good to know a grown-up has your back.

"No. No. No." Emily shakes her head vehemently. "You can't tell her. She'll go to the police."

I consider that. She might. She might not. My mother's not the most predictable person on the planet. Except when it comes to deadbeat men, and even that could be changing.

"You have to promise you won't tell her. Or anyone. This is about Tasha's life." Emily's face is so white, she's fading into the drywall.

I immediately feel sick at the thought of Tasha in the forest with Michael. "Okay."

Emily runs a shaky hand through her hair. "You have to promise."

"I promise."

My phone chirps with a text from Shirlee.

Call me!

"You want me to take any of your stuff now?" I say to Emily.

"Sure." She walks up the stairs to hand me a couple of bags filled with clothes. "I'll come late tonight."

"Watch out for Mrs. Burns. She's already seen you and thought you were me." I stand.

Shirlee texts. I messed everything up.

Butterflies fighting in my stomach, I hug the wall at the side of the house, then hustle to the sidewalk. When I turn the corner, I call her.

"I totally messed up," she wails as soon as she answers the phone, "and Jennifer called me on it. I mentioned his mother telling him to do something in a text. Apparently, she died. I kind of forgot I don't know anything about this guy. I'm so sorry."

"No worries. It could still end up okay." I jog up the driveway to my house.

"No, I blew it for us. Jennifer never replied. She knows something's weird."

"Where are you?" I set Emily's bags on the top step to the basement and close the door. "Want to give me your phone for the night? In case she texts him later?"

"Sure. I'm at home. Although I don't see her doing that. I bet she never texts him again." Shirlee sighs. "And Jennifer'll keep picking on us."

I change into shorts and a T-shirt and lace up my running shoes. I might as well get a workout with all this bouncing from house to house.

It's not till I've been running for about ten minutes and my mind is clear that I realize I never asked Emily how she's getting evidence on Michael. I hit my forehead with my palm. I'll ask her when she's back at my place.

Jogging onto Shirlee's street, I see a little hunched figure on the curb in the middle of the cul-de-sac. The way the sun's slanting next to her, leaving her in a big wedge of shadow, Shirlee looks like a poster for depression.

When I reach her, she passes me her phone in silence.

R you @ home or skool? Jennifer sent.

????? Again, from Jennifer.

I want to see you. She texted after still getting no response from Michael.

@ doc appt, Shirlee finally texted.

R u sick?

Prob just sprained ankle, but my mom's making me get it checked out

What???? I thot ur mom died????

Meant dad. Too much pain. Going into xray.

"You handled that well," I say. "I love the 'too much pain.'"

She makes a face. "See how Jennifer hasn't answered? *She* doesn't love the 'too much pain.'"

"Maybe she figured out someone pranked her. And maybe she'll never text this number again." I jog in place. "But we tried."

"If only she'd trashed Alyssa and Danielle, so we'd have

something to use against her." Shirlee's chin hits her chest. "Instead we're still at her mercy."

"At least we didn't get caught." I smile at her, but inside I have the same defeated feeling. It's like training really hard for a race, only to trip and fall and come in last. Except this is more important.

Shirlee shuffles into her house, and I continue my workout. Now I'm even more determined to beat Jennifer at the first invite.

I'm probably fifteen minutes into my run when Shirlee's phone buzzes. I jog in place and pull it out of my pocket. It's Jennifer.

> Sorry. My mom took my phone cause I wasn't doing homework. Annoying. U still @ doc?

> Yeah. So much pain. I really do love the "pain" line.

> I have surprise 4 u. I'll leave it on ur porch 4 wen u get home.

> Why don't u give it to me Sat instead?

> Saturday?

> @ bonfire. I'll meet u there.

> Cool. Will u sit with me and my friends?

> Sure. Jennifer must be swooning right about now.

Wat if ur on crutches?

U can help me right? Jennifer may have just
swooned herself onto the ground.

Of course I'll help, silly. Just left ur house. Look
on porch wen u get home.

I turn so abruptly there's probably smoke wisping from
the rubber soles of my shoes. I race toward Sparrow. Full-
on race. She can't bump into Michael. She can't. She can't.
She can't. He can't find the surprise. He can't. He can't. He
can't.

I skid around the corner, breathing hard enough to pop
a rib. I'm slick with sweat. I slow to a walk.

Sparrow's quiet, with no one around and only a couple
of cars parked by the curb.

From the bottom of the walkway to Michael's house,
I can see a red gift bag hanging on the front doorknob.
I stride toward it with fake confidence. This neighborhood might have their own Mrs. Burns. I'm swinging my
arms and walking tall. As if I have every right to the
gift bag.

What's in it? I push apart the tissue paper. An Oily Artichokes key chain. I grasp the handles of the bag and step
off the concrete porch.

Suddenly a car screeches around the corner and
squeals to a stop in front of number 70. The garage door
rolls up.

I'm totally exposed with nowhere to hide. No bushes. No trees. No porch furniture.

Michael explodes out, slamming his door. He scowls, his eyebrows an angry slash across his forehead. "Who are you?"

My mind is as blank as a yard of new snow.

With cold eyes, he takes in the gift bag and my running outfit. "You're from the middle school? Another friend of Jennifer's? Get lost. And tell Jennifer to get lost." The words shoot out like bullets.

I nod. I edge down the steps. I'm shaking like the temperature's dipped to subarctic degrees.

Michael disappears into the garage. The door thuds down on the driveway.

As I pass his car, my fingers light on fire with tingles. I glance inside. The guy's a major slob. The backseat's covered with fast-food containers, a balled-up sweatshirt, a pack of cigarettes, a travel coffee mug. And tiny sparkles. More sparkles than I've seen in ages. As if someone broke open a jumbo-size vial of glitter and sprinkled.

I glance at the house. No sign of life. I tug open the back door and slip in.

Keeping low, I grab the three items with the brightest sparkles. I'll read the memories at home. I don't actually have a death wish.

My elbow's pushing down on the door handle when the garage door creaks open. Footsteps approach. The trunk pops up.

I flatten myself on the gross floor of trash, lying as still as possible. One look through the window, and I'm busted. My heart hurls itself loudly against my rib cage.

The trunk slams shut. A cell phone rings. "Yeah?" Michael says. Footsteps fade as he moves away. The second the garage door bumps down, I'm out of the car, taking off like I'm powered by a rocket launcher.

CHAPTER 28

I sit on my bed and take a few deep, yoga-like breaths. The three objects from his car are on my nightstand: an empty soda cup, a pair of sunglasses, and a disposable glove.

I start with the sunglasses, balancing them in my palm and staring till I'm cross-eyed. It's a quick memory of Michael punching the car dash and swearing. I watch the memory a few times, looking for details, but don't get anything very helpful. He's wearing a light jacket, so it's fall or spring. It must have happened recently, because he looks the same. The swearing is just a string of bad language. No details about why he's losing it.

Next I try the disposable glove. I get nothing. I try a few

different ways, with the candle, without the candle, hand open, hand closed. Zip. Zero. I give up.

The soda cup has the brightest, pointiest sparkle of the three objects. I wrap my hands around it, lacing my fingers together. I lean back on my pillow.

Michael's crouched down, gesturing to a dog. "Come here, Pes. Come here, boy." On the ground next to him sits a grocery bag.

The dog, medium-size, a mixture of breeds, has deep brown eyes like Levi. Pes sits and stares at Michael, sniffs the air and whines. He doesn't budge.

"You don't want to be my friend?" Michael pulls a piece of raw meat from the bag. "That's okay. We don't have to be friends for this to work." He waves the meat.

Pes sniffs some more and licks his lips. He walks in circles but keeps his distance.

Michael tosses the hunk of meat. It lands at Pes's feet.

The dog sniffs it, turns it over with his paw, sniffs again, then chews thoughtfully. The whole time, he watches Michael out of the corner of his eye.

Michael throws another piece of meat.

Same cautious scenario.

By the fourth chunk, Pes pounces and goes for it.

Michael takes a plastic bottle from the bag. The label says RACUMIN: RAT POISON. *He pours blue liquid onto the next piece of meat and lets it soak in.*

When he lobs it to Pes, the dog doesn't hesitate. He chomps on the meat, downing it in seconds.

Michael feeds the dog more and more tainted meat. Pes eats it all.

I crush the cup and throw it in my trash can. Then I wipe my eyes. Michael poisoned Tasha's dog.

Michael White is the scariest person I've ever met.

"Raine," Mom calls from the kitchen. "Dinner."

While my mom's carrying bowls of chili over to the counter, I hug Levi, then feed her, adding a few treats to her kibble.

I force down a couple of spoonfuls of chili, but I'm just not hungry. I can't get the evilness of Michael out of my brain.

"Are you feeling sick?" my mom asks, buttering a slice of French bread.

"Just tired. I'm going to bed."

I set my alarm for one in the morning. Surprisingly, I actually fall asleep. Of course, I have nightmares about fires and alarm clocks and a dog and blue poison and a guy with soulless eyes.

At 12:59, before my alarm has a chance to go off, I jolt awake. I pull on a sweatshirt, grab Shirlee's phone, and head to the kitchen.

I crack the door to the basement stairs. Emily's bags are still on the top step where I set them. She's not here yet.

Dunking chocolate chip cookies in milk, I read the texts I missed from Jennifer. They're a bunch of questions. Is Michael's ankle broken or sprained? Did he find the surprise? Did he like it? Why isn't he replying?

Sprained. Sleeping lots. Only woke for more
pain pills. Key chain is epic. I press send.

A key turns in the back door lock. Emily tiptoes in.

"Emily," I whisper loudly. "I'm in the kitchen."

She peers around the corner. "Where's your mom?"

"In bed, zonked out on sleeping pills." I bite into another cookie. "You want something to eat?"

"Sure." Emily slips out of her backpack and drops it to the floor along with the sleeping bag and a couple more bags of stuff.

"Chili?" I open the fridge and pull out leftovers.

"Sure," she says again.

"You can sit." I scoop chili into a bowl and nuke it.

Emily perches on the edge of a barstool, looking awkward and out of place. She must be starving, because she digs into the chili like it's gourmet. Which it's definitely not.

This whole situation is so beyond weird that I just have to roll with it. I'm sitting in my kitchen, in the middle of the night, heating up chili for a girl everyone thinks is dead but who's actually living in my basement because she's collecting evidence to convict a high school arsonist who threatened her sister if she goes to the cops. It doesn't even fit in a sentence.

"Exactly how are you getting evidence on Michael?" I ask as she shakes Parmesan cheese onto her chili.

"I'm following him online. He created this online group

for teenage arsonists. They all brag about their fires and exchange tips and have contests. Very sick and creepy." She blows on a spoonful of chili. "I go out at night for the Internet. I can get on with my laptop in the Bean's parking lot."

"You have a laptop here?" I say, surprised.

"Tasha brought mine over," Emily explains. "I have my cell phone, too. No service, but I can still use the camera and listen to my music."

"Why aren't the police following him online, too?" I say, trying to process this weird situation.

"They'd never find him. He's using a chat room through the high school." She tears the crust off a slice of French bread.

"Would a teacher find it?"

"No way," she says with confidence. "They wouldn't even be looking for it."

"But you found him."

"I hacked in," she says nonchalantly, the way I say "I walked the dog." "I'm not showing the police. I don't trust them." She dunks her bread in the chili. "They already messed up investigating Michael once. Plus he's a pretty good hacker. He'd be able to tell if they were cyberspying."

"What's he saying online?" I ask.

"They have this contest going. 'Bigger and Better.' You have to one-up the guy before you. Set a 'better' fire. On Saturday, Michael's burning down two buildings: a shed and a cabin."

"Where?"

"There's a motel sign out on Highway Twenty. The path behind it leads up a hill. If you go one way, you come to a ravine. That's where Jennifer and those guys left me. The other way goes farther into the woods where the cabin and shed are."

"He chose that cabin because . . . ?" I ask.

"He hates the guy whose family owns it. Hates him."

"You already have some evidence?" I ask.

"I've got screenshots of all his posts. On Friday, he'll set up for the fire with cushions and newspapers and gasoline. He's using a timer, an alarm clock again, to start the flames. He'll be at the bonfire, nowhere near the scene, while the fire takes off. I'll go out Saturday during the day and take photos of the setup. I'll give the posts and photos to the police. Together, they're strong evidence. The police can work with the fire department to disarm the clock and prevent the fire."

Emily sounds so reasonable and organized. Like she's planning a simple field trip. But Michael White is dangerous. Very dangerous.

CHAPTER 29

$\mathscr{I}$ arrive at school to find Shirlee pacing around the flag-pole like a prisoner in a jail cell. "What's going on?" she asks me.

"Read the texts," I say, giving her back her phone.

She reads, chewing on her bottom lip. "You intercepted the gift? Weren't you scared?"

"Definitely," I admit.

The bell rings, and we walk toward the main entrance. I spot Jennifer and her girls inside, waiting for one of us. "Go in the side doors," I say to Shirlee.

"Jennifer?" Panic colors her voice.

"Go, go. I got this one." And it's true. When Jennifer

and the others start the *KleptoRainia* thing, I almost don't realize it's going on. They're so nothing compared to Michael. Like a few drops of summer rain compared to a monsoon.

At lunch, Torie slides her tray across the table, then follows it. "Hugh and Avalon broke up," she says. Her eyes shine with excitement.

"I never got what he saw in her to begin with," Sydney says.

"She's really good at video games." Willow picks up her sandwich.

Torie snorts. "Do you find something nice to say about everyone?"

Willow reddens.

"Except possibly you, Torie." Sydney laughs.

"Avalon's failing Spanish," a girl from the other end of the table says. "She never does her homework. As in not once since the beginning of the year."

"I think I'm failing Spanish, and that's *with* doing my homework. Lopez is the worst teacher ever," Sydney replies. "Who wants my pudding?"

I don't mention Avalon and the mystery guy at the elementary school. Hugh might be in the know, but doesn't want to broadcast it to all of Yielding Middle. And if he doesn't know, I don't want to be responsible for starting that rumor mill.

Shirlee passes me her phone under the table.

My grlfriends r getting on my nerves. Jennifer texts from across the room.

What r they doing? I hit send.

Saying mean things abt u.

Not cool.

Alyssa's so jealous of me. She has no self-esteem. She photoshops her selfies to look thinner and get rid of her zits.

Whats with the other girl?

Rele stupid. Its embarrassing when danielle talks. Shes failing everything. She eats too much. No self-control, Jennifer texts.

Hang in there. See you tomorro at the bonfire babe.

"Screenshot these," I say to Shirlee under my breath. "Email them to me."

I stand when the end-of-lunch bell rings, gathering up my trash.

"You heard what I said about Hugh and Avalon." Torie slurps the last of her chocolate milk. "Now's your chance, Raine."

"I'm not interested in him," I say.

"Puh-lease." Torie rolls her eyes to the top of her head. "Like anyone's buying that."

"Don't be so pushy, Torie," Willow says. "Wow. I just said something not nice."

"Hugh doesn't look like he's crying over the breakup. He and Garrett are cracking up at their table." Sydney pops the last of an Oreo in her mouth.

I refuse to turn around and look.

"I'm leaving," I announce.

"Wait for me." Shirlee starts positioning her plastic containers in her lunch bag.

The hall is crowded, and we're dodging people like we're riding bumper cars at the fair. Even when a guy crashes right into her, Shirlee can't turn off her smile. "Those texts are so perfect."

"I agree."

I stop at my locker for my afternoon books.

"By the way, hooking up with Hugh goes along with your horoscope," Shirlee says, walking away before I can answer.

The rest of my classes go okay, even better than okay. In English, Mrs. Hughes hands back last week's test on *The Call of the Wild,* which I seriously rocked, including the essay question. When Mrs. Woodford calls on me in science, I'm able to answer her question about electrons and noble gases. Mr. Magee shows a movie for the entire period of film. And I'm not exaggerating when I say I run like the wind in practice. Coach gives me the biggest thumbs-up ever. Torie, Sydney, and Willow calculate what I can buy with the prize gift certificate from the upcoming invite. Jennifer is furious, throwing stuff in her locker hard enough to dent the metal.

That evening, after my mom goes to bed and the house falls silent and dark, I start thinking about tomorrow. Saturday. The street fair. The bonfire. Emily sneaking out to take incriminating pictures of Michael's arson setup in the woods.

So much can mess up. If Emily's timing is off, Michael could spot her. I shudder. The firefighters and police could refuse to take Emily seriously. Or they could set her evidence aside because they're busy. Then the cabin fire would rage out of control.

I sit in bed and play mindless video games on my computer, hoping to numb my brain enough that I fall asleep.

Around midnight, Torie texts.

> I get why ur not interested in hugh.

> ???

> Bec ur interested in a high skool guy, Torie replies.

My stomach begins swirling.

> ??? I text back.

> He was across street after skool today, asking ppl abt u while we were @ practice. I heard he's cute. Has an Oily Artichokes t shirt like you.

Asking them what? The swirling speeds up,
throwing my dinner to the walls of my stomach.

Ur name, where you live.

Did ppl tell him?

Of course!

I think I'm going to throw up. Why did Michael want
my address? To torch my house? I have to tell Emily. She
has to get enough on him tomorrow to get him thrown
in jail.

I can hear my mom snoring softly as I head out of my
bedroom. I knock on the basement door. No answer.
I open it. "Emily. Emily," I whisper-call, not wanting to
freak her out. I flip up the light switch. I walk down three
steps and crane my neck to see around the corner. Her
sleeping area is empty. Her laptop power cord is plugged
into the wall, but the laptop is gone. Emily's left to do her
cyberspying at the Jitter Bean's parking lot.

I camp out in the living room, watching reruns, determined to catch her when she returns.

After a couple of shows, I go to the kitchen and stare out
the window over the sink, watching for Emily. Mrs. Burns's
house is shrouded in black. With no breeze, the bushes,
the tree, every blade of grass all stand perfectly still.

And then my eye latches onto a small red circle of light
across the street. It moves slowly in a line from lower to
higher, then stops. Then it moves down low again, stops,

then moves higher, then stops. From hip height to head, then back to hip. A little red, glowing circle.

Someone is standing across the street, smoking a cigarette. Who? Michael? The person's next to the streetlight, just outside the arc of light, protected by the shadows.

I watch from the safety of my kitchen, from the safety of the darkness, almost hypnotized by the moving, glowing tip. From hip to mouth to hip.

Then the red tip falls to the sidewalk. The person steps forward to grind out the glow with the toe of a shoe.

It *is* Michael. He steps back into the shadow, invisible again.

"Stay away, Emily," I whisper. "Stay away." I wipe my clammy hands on my pajama bottoms.

Michael hangs out a little longer. Then there's a blue flare from a lighter as he lights another cigarette. He starts walking along the sidewalk, in the opposite direction of the Jitter Bean. He stops, throws back his head, sucks in, and blows smoke rings. He begins walking again.

I breathe out a huge sigh of relief. He's leaving without seeing Emily.

A couple of houses down the street, he stops, does the smoke-ring thing and looks around, checking the neighborhood one more time.

Suddenly, he freezes, like he's been Tasered, a look of total disbelief on his face.

Picking her way home from the Jitter Bean, Emily's balancing on the curb. She stops directly under a streetlight.

You can tell by the smile on her face that she's lost in her own thoughts, happy to be outside, even in the dead of night.

Michael backs into the shadow of a tree.

Emily circles away from Mrs. Burns's motion light and skips across our lawn. I hear the soft thump of her footsteps on the hard dirt as she passes under the kitchen window. Then the back door creaks. She's in. The lock clicks.

Head down, Michael quickly crosses the street and follows the same path as Emily. Watching through the smallest possible crack in the blinds, I see him pause and listen at the side of our house, a hand on the bricks. He's like a predator tracking. I almost expect him to sniff. When he gets close to the window, my heart plugs up my throat. I can barely catch a breath.

Emily enters the kitchen. "The light's on in the living room."

"Shhh." I point at the window. "Michael."

Her face drains of blood.

Michael vanishes from sight.

Next we hear the rattle of a doorknob as he tries to open the back door. There's a thud as he pushes on the locked door. Then silence. Then footsteps past the kitchen. Then another rattle as he tries the porch doorknob.

Emily and I are shaking.

Finally, through the kitchen window, I watch Michael walk across the yard and veer onto the street.

"What was he doing here?" Emily asks.

I give her the quick version of how Shirlee and I are getting back at Jennifer, that Michael saw me at his house and then asked people at school about me. "But why come here? And hang out across the street, smoking? Why even check up on me at school? I'm nobody to him. Nobody." With each sentence, my voice squeaks higher. "Is he going to burn my house down?"

Emily chews on her bottom lip. "Maybe he didn't have a definite plan. But you made him uneasy. Those are some weird coincidences. You were at his front door. You know Jennifer. You live in the house of the girl who knew he was setting fires." She chews some more. "Did he think I left a diary behind? That you actually knew something?"

"He's so evil and creepy."

"And now he knows I'm still alive." Emily starts to cry.

CHAPTER 30

$\mathcal{S}$aturday morning finds me up early and in the passenger seat of our truck.

Apparently, in a parallel life, I agreed to help my mother at her property management's street fair booth. She wouldn't take no for an answer.

We squeal into the Jitter Bean's parking lot. "Want a hot chocolate?"

"No. I'm good," I say. What's Michael planning? Will he go after Tasha?

"Come in and choose a doughnut." Mom squeezes my shoulder.

I follow her. Will he go after Emily? Will he burn my house down?

Hugh's behind the counter, helping his dad with the morning rush. He's very wide awake. "Street fair volunteer?" he asks, glancing at my mother's T-shirt.

"Absolutely." She beams.

"The only decent parts are the bonfire and the fireworks," he says cheerfully to me. "I put an extra one in for you. For doing your civic duty." He hands me the bag of doughnuts.

Just hearing the word *bonfire* sends my pulse skyrocketing. Will Emily get enough evidence to convince the police to go after Michael? Will Michael concentrate on his original plan of setting the cabin and shed on fire during the bonfire?

"Hugh seems like a nice guy," my mom says, glancing quickly at me as she pulls into traffic.

"Uh-huh," I reply. How long will Michael leave Emily, Tasha, and me alone? Long enough that he gets locked up? When we get to her company's booth, my mom introduces me to Nancy, the other volunteer and her coworker. "As soon as you're finished eating, we're putting you on the fortune wheel," my mom says.

I spend the next three hours spinning a heavy wooden wheel for kids wanting a small free prize.

"My arms are falling out of their sockets," I finally complain to my mom as she hands out rubber bracelets.

"I think Raine's done enough," Nancy says. "My son'll be here in five. He can man the wheel."

The drive home is filled with Mom gushing about the

street fair and Yielding and community. "This really is a great town, isn't it?"

Except for Michael White. And Jennifer and her gang. But especially Michael White. I rub my biceps. "I need a shower and some Advil."

She drops me off and heads back downtown. I'm almost at the porch steps when Mrs. Burns comes hurtling across the lawn, all body parts jiggling, eyeballs bulging. Even the sparkle on her shoulder is shaking. I don't bother to reach for it. Who wants to see the memories of a cranky, old busybody?

"What shenanigans are you up to now?" she demands.

"Nothing." I put a foot on the first step.

"Who was that boy over here this morning?"

"What?" The blood in my veins turns cold.

"He walked around your house, looked through all the windows, then knocked at the back door." She glares at me. "The door opened, and he went in. Then out came the two of you, arms around each other. You were wrapped in a large coat. And off you went together." She wags a finger. "Something illegal's going on."

Emily left with Michael?

In a panic, I race up the porch stairs and into the house.

Mrs. Burns's mouth is probably starting a lecture on rudeness. I don't hang around to find out.

I change my shoes, grab water, and take off.

It's the toughest five-mile run I've ever done. Each step feels like I'm in a nightmare, running underwater. Did

Michael take Emily to the cabin? I don't know where else to look.

At the Motel 6 sign, I veer left off the highway and start climbing the hill. About halfway up, I find his car. A little hope. At least I'm at the right place. I look in. No Emily. A large man's coat lies on the backseat. Where is she? Is she hurt? Is she alive? Maybe there's a sparkle inside the car that will tell me what's going on. I try the doors. Locked.

I make my way into the woods. When I spot the cabin, I crouch down by a tree at the edge of the clearing and look around. A stack of newspapers next to a cushion next to newspapers next to a cushion forms a checkered path that snakes from the shed to the cabin. It's almost pretty. The wind picks up, ruffling the newspapers.

Suddenly Michael appears, backing out of the shed. He's lugging a plastic drum. When he tips the drum and starts soaking cushions and newspapers, I can smell the gasoline.

I pull out my phone. No service. I'm afraid to backtrack down the hill to get bars. Michael will see me. Instead, I begin taping.

When the container is empty, he drops it in the middle of the yard and walks down the hill. To leave? Because the timer's set for tonight and ready to spark a blaze?

Where is Emily?

I stay in the woods, dashing from tree to tree in a wide circle till I reach the cabin. I peer in the windows. No Emily.

The shed doors are still open. Is she in there? Tied up? Knocked out? Left to burn to death? Already dead?

I sprint around the cabin and gaze into the shed.

I stifle a cry. Like an empty sack, Emily's crumpled in a heap on the floor. Duct tape is wrapped around her hands and ankles and stretches across her mouth. Her eyes are closed.

I glance over my shoulder. No sign of Michael. Has he left?

"Emily," I whisper. "Emily."

Her eyes flutter open, then go wide, wide like saucers. She shakes her head and makes high-pitched squealing noises.

There's a scuffling behind me.

I turn just as Michael lunges.

He's like a truck crashing into me.

I fall heavily into the shed.

Pain shoots into my head above my eye.

The shed doors slam shut.

CHAPTER 31

I lie there for a minute, blinking. It's dark. A little light fights its way in through the small window. I don't let myself think about spiders.

There's a loud click outside. We're locked in.

My head hurts. I keep blinking. What's getting in my eye? I raise a hand to my eyebrow, then hold my hand up to the dim stream of light. Blood. There's a huge gash above my eyebrow. It's dripping blood into my eye.

Beside me, Emily's making frustrated grunts. She kicks me, then shakes her bound arms and legs.

I pull myself slowly to my knees, a hand on the ground to stay steady. I work on pulling the tape off Emily's hands, stopping every so often to wipe the blood from my eye.

When her hands are free, Emily holds the edge of the tape covering her mouth, closes her eyes and rips. She squeals. "That really hurts," she whimpers, pressing fingers against her lips.

Under her hoodie, Emily wriggles until she gets her T-shirt off and hands it to me. "Hold this against your eyebrow."

With the light from my phone, I grab a shovel and a hoe from the other side of the shed. Emily finishes untaping her feet.

I give the shovel to Emily, and we start whacking at the doors. When nothing gives, we wedge the tools in the gap where the doors meet, trying to pry them open.

They don't budge.

Huffing and puffing, Emily leans on the long handle of the shovel. "This isn't working."

With the metal end of the hoe, I smash the window. "I want to see what's going on outside."

Carefully, I stick my head through the opening.

Michael stands inches away, staring at me.

I jump back, like I was shocked, and a jagged piece of glass scrapes into my neck.

"Let us out." My voice trembles.

"Yeah, right." He walks away, wiping his hands on his jeans.

The panic in me bubbles and expands until it threatens to blow off my head. I go back to attacking the doors with the hoe.

When Emily doesn't help, I shine the phone light in her face. She's sniffing.

Then I smell it, too.

Smoke.

Long, slender blue flames stretch up the back wall.

Michael didn't wait for tonight and the bonfire.

Emily jumps next to me, like somehow together we can fight the fire beast. We can't.

The flames turn from pretty blue to angry orange and red. The fire crackles louder and louder. The temperature in the shed is rising fast.

Hot smoke billows and swoops down my throat and into my lungs.

Emily dives for the floor and pulls me down with her. "Stay below the fumes and cover your mouth." She pulls up on the bottom of her hoodie.

I slap her T-shirt over my mouth.

The flames on the back wall curl up to the roof. If we don't get out soon, we'll be burned alive.

I cough. My eyes sting. I wipe sweat from my forehead.

"We're going to die," Emily whispers. "From carbon monoxide poisoning or from the flames."

Really? This is it? No more moves with my mother? No more Levi? No more running? No first kiss? No prom? No more sparkles?

Sparkles.

I take a breath from near the floor, hold it, then stand and poke my head out the window.

A combination lock is threaded through the door handles.

I drop down. Breathe in. Hold it. Stand.

I stick my head and arm through the window, stretching for the lock. My fingers bump it. There's a faint sparkle. I tap it with my fingertips, rolling it along my fingers to my palm. I close my hand and my eyes.

I need this memory. More than I've needed any memory before. More than I've needed anything in my entire life.

Numbers leap into my mind.

33-7-41.

The combination to open the lock.

"Breathe, Raine," Emily says hoarsely from the ground.

I fall to the floor.

"What are you doing?" Emily asks.

"Opening the lock," I choke out, then breathe and stagger to my feet.

I squeeze my head and arm through the window again.

The wind gusts, and flames suddenly dance across the yard on the path of cushions and newspapers.

On my tiptoes, I stretch my arm, reaching, reaching for the lock.

33-7-41.

There's a roaring crash as a wall falls behind us. Burning debris flies through the air.

The back of my knee flares in heat. I scream.

Emily smothers the flames on my leg with her hoodie.

My fingers strain for the dial.

And get it. The lock's hot.

I twist it to thirty-three, spin it left past seven, then turn it all the way around to seven again.

The fire rages and moans. It wants us. I can't smell anymore. Every breath hurts. Every cough hurts. I'm dizzy.

Right to forty-one.

The lock pops open. I shove it through the door handles. It hits the ground.

Emily slumps against me.

I pull her by her armpits. Then, with the weight of both our bodies, I crash into the hot doors. They fall open.

I drag Emily out and across the clearing.

We collapse onto the dirt.

CHAPTER 32

*T*here's a sharp rap on the door before a hospital worker walks in with a meal tray.

My mom's asleep in the chair next to my bed. Her arms are flung out like she's flying, and her bangs are damp and stuck to her forehead. She looks like a little kid.

"Breakfast." The worker sets the tray on the stand next to my bed.

"Thanks," I say.

Our voices nudge my mom awake.

"Were you here all night?" I ask her.

She stands and stretches. "Yeah."

I didn't expect that, and it makes me feel safe, like I'm

wrapped in a fuzzy blanket. "Want some?" I wave at the tray.

"Just the coffee." She reaches for the mug.

I'm surprisingly hungry and start shoveling in rubbery scrambled eggs and limp slices of bacon.

Watching me with serious eyes, my mom sips her coffee.

I drain my carton of milk, then set my fork on the empty plate. "I wonder if I'm getting out today or tomorrow."

"Tomorrow. The doctor stopped by earlier." My mom places her mug on a corner of the tray, then wheels the small table against the wall. She perches on the side of my bed. "We need to talk, Raine."

She usually avoids heavy, emotional conversations. I chew on my bottom lip.

"You kept some really big secrets." She pauses. "It's one thing not to tell me when a project is due or that you bombed a test. But this"—her eyes well up with tears—"was way, way beyond that. This was so dangerous that it's amazing things didn't go very wrong. You and Emily could easily have—" She buries her face in her hands.

"I'm sorry," I say. And I mean it. "I'm really sorry. We didn't know how dangerous it was going to get. That Michael would get Emily. That he'd lock us in the shed and set it on fire."

She looks at me. "Why didn't you tell me about Emily?"

"Emily was worried you'd go to the police. Then Michael would find out she was still around and he'd get

Tasha. That's why Emily left our house with him. He said it was either her or Tasha."

She waits for me to continue.

"I just promised . . . ," I trail off lamely.

"There are some promises you can't make," my mom says softly. "You have to say no when you're asked."

I nod. It's the best I can do because my throat is so tight, it's trapping the words.

She grabs hold of me and hugs me hard. We're both crying, my hot tears streaming down her neck, her hot tears streaming down mine.

"You have to have faith in me, Raine," she chokes out. "I'm really doing my best to be here for you. To make Yielding the fresh start you deserve. Sure, I'll make mistakes. You'll make mistakes, too. Your grandmother would've made mistakes. But I have your best interests at heart. I'm coming from a place of love. That's what you have to trust."

I cry harder. She cries harder. We hang on to each other, crying for all the scary things that could've gone wrong but didn't, and for all the wonderful things that are going right.

Finally we pull apart. We wipe our eyes and blow our noses with tissues from the box on my nightstand.

"So we agree we're going to talk more?" my mom asks, her hands on my shoulders. "And hang out together more?"

I nod.

"You okay if I go into work for a while? We're having a

move-in special at one of the apartments this weekend, and it'll be a zoo."

"Sure."

She turns at the door. "A boy stopped by the house to ask about you."

I go still, waiting for the name.

"Lou? Drew? The coffee shop guy."

"Hugh?" I say.

"That's the one."

"The worst thing about Yielding Hospital is the Internet connection," I say in answer to Shirlee's question. "Although the mystery lunch today was suspicious. Might've been worm. Or lizard skin."

"Yuck." Shirlee sets her laptop bag on the floor. "Is Emily still here?"

"No. She already got discharged because she has less of a heat rash on her face."

"Did she go home with her family?" Shirlee asks.

"Yeah."

"I cannot even imagine that reunion."

"There was a lot of hugging and crying," I say. "Emily's mom couldn't stop touching her. Her dad, who doesn't seem like a very happy guy, was literally grinning from ear to ear."

"Is Emily coming back to Yielding Middle?"

I shake my head. "They're moving. Her dad got a job with the same company my mom works for. But in Albany."

"Maybe that's better for her," Shirlee says. "She'll get a chance to start over."

It's probably true for Emily, but not for me. I'm glad to be staying in the same house and going to the same school. I'm maxed out on starting over.

Shirlee leans close, scrutinizing my face. "Your rash doesn't look too bad."

"Underneath this cream, my face is shiny and red. There's a line of blisters across my forehead. It's not pretty." I point at my eyebrow. "Stitches."

"Will it all heal okay?"

"That's what the doctor promised." With three fingers, I show a Scout's honor.

"And Emily's obviously in good shape?"

"Yeah, although she got more smoke inhalation than me and blew out her mucous membranes. She sounds like a wounded animal when she snores. That's how her dad described it."

Shirlee laughs. "Your mom said you hurt your knee, too?"

I nod. "The back of my knee is actually burned, to the point I can't bend it. I'm not looking forward to telling the coach I'm out for the rest of the season."

"Torie's going to tell him at practice tomorrow."

I push the button that makes the bed sit up. "So what happened at the bonfire with Jennifer?"

"She was wearing new clothes, tons of makeup, telling everyone to leave room for her"—Shirlee makes air quotation marks—" 'high school' boyfriend to sit next to her. When he didn't show up, she texted. And texted and texted."

"What'd you do?"

"She texted me. I texted you. Neither one of us got replies. It went on like that for a while."

I make a sorry face. "I didn't get your texts till it was too late."

"It's fine. I just never answered her."

"You *never* answered?" I repeat.

"Nope." Shirlee gives a satisfied smile. "Eventually, she made up a big lie and said Michael really wanted to be at the bonfire with her, but had to go back to the doctor's because he was in so much pain and it turned out his ankle was badly broken not just sprained." Shirlee mimics Jennifer talking fast with no spaces between words.

"I wonder what she'll be like in school this week."

"Bad." Shirlee sighs. "I'm sure she'll leave you alone. The whole school knows how you found Emily and how you two helped catch the arsonist. She'll try to convince everyone that the arsonist's a different Michael White." Shirlee gives a short laugh. "But there's no reason for her to stop picking on me."

"We'll give her a reason." I slowly swing my legs over the side of the bed. "The Internet's better in the lounge."

Shirlee hangs out with me for the rest of the afternoon, and we put together a YouTube video about Jennifer. The title? "The Mean Girl's Going Down." We find online photos of Jennifer, Alyssa, Danielle, and Michael. The opening's a close-up photo of Jennifer, followed by fingers tapping on a phone. We upload all her texts. We show how desperate she is for Michael to like her. But how she winds up alone. And how she's really alone, because after Michael's photo, we put handcuffs and then the juvenile hall in Albany. We follow all this with the mean texts about Alyssa and Danielle in a segment called "Oops. Mean Girl Trash-Talks Her Friends." Of course we set the video to great music. Voilà.

We upload our work of art to YouTube with privacy settings. At this point, only Jennifer, Shirlee, and I can view the video.

"How should we let her know about this?" I ask.

"Text her? Email? Facebook message?" Shirlee shrugs.

In the end, we use all of the above to give Jennifer the YouTube link and a message saying the next time she bugs either Shirlee or me, we're taking off the privacy setting.

Shirlee's mom texts that she's in the parking lot.

Shirlee gives me a light hug. "You're the bravest person I know. I can't imagine how scary it must've been in the shed."

"It was the scariest thing that's ever happened to me," I admit. "But I also think Emily and I got lucky. Like with that hiker calling nine-one-one about the fire. With the shed combusting after we got out. With not getting hit by any of the stuff flying out of the shed." I shudder. "That whole scenario could've been so bad."

"And the arsonist forgetting to actually lock the lock," Shirlee says. "That's what they said on the news."

"Yeah, that, too."

"To me, you have courage. I'm not just talking about the fire and Michael White." She taps her laptop. "Jennifer, too."

"Thanks."

"You're sure you'll be ready for school in a couple of days?" Shirlee says.

"I'm sure I won't be ready," I say, "but I'll be there—me and my bright red puffy face."

CHAPTER 33

 $\mathcal{M}$ y first day back, my mom drives me to school. I stand alone on the corner, looking across at Yielding Middle. Same boring red brick. Same horizontal stripes of windows. Same pathetic cougar mascot painted above the front doors.

A lot has changed since I stood in this same place the day of registration. I found a missing girl. I helped catch an arsonist. I know my teachers. I recognize lots of students, like Garrett, who's hanging out by the flagpole, shooting spitballs at the girls walking by. I have a few friends.

Still, my stomach is heavy with nerves. It sucks to limp into school, wearing a face that looks like it baked too long in a tanning booth.

I reach into my pocket and pull out the little dented silver heart. I watch the sparkles, glinting, waiting for me to read them. I start closing my fingers over them.

"Raine."

I jump, and the heart clatters to the sidewalk.

Hugh bends over and picks it up.

"Thanks," I say, sliding it into my pocket.

"How're you feeling?" he asks.

"Okay, I guess. Considering."

"That's some pretty crazy stuff you've been through." He looks straight at me while he talks, not flinching at the sight of my face.

"Seriously."

"But just because you got an arsonist off the streets and reunited a missing girl back with her family, don't think that gets you off the hook with the film project."

I laugh. "Meaning what?"

"Tomorrow night. Mario's," he says. "I know you've got a busy schedule. I heard the *Today* show wants an appearance from you and Emily. And the president's sending Air Force One to fly you to the White House. But I bargained hard to get my brother to drive us to Mario's."

"How hard?" I ask.

"I'm on trash duty, and I have to do his laundry for an entire month. Plus I have to wash and vacuum his car."

"Tomorrow night works." I step off the curb. "The other stuff's just a rumor, anyway."

"Too bad." He steps down after me.

We walk across the street and the front lawn.

"Don't even think about it," I say to Garrett.

He salutes me with his empty pen. "I wasn't going to, Raine. I don't spitball war heroes."

I roll my eyes.

Hugh stays with Garrett, and I hobble over to where Shirlee's standing by the front entrance.

"They're in there. Just on the other side of the doors," she says nervously. "Did you ever hear back from her? What if she hasn't seen the video?"

"My mom and I stopped at the Jitter Bean on the way to school. I checked our YouTube video. Ten views. Have you been watching it?" I ask.

"Not since the hospital."

"Then she's seen it. Multiple times." I grab the door handle. "She's figured out she was texting us, not Michael. She knows we're serious about going public." I pull on the door. "Jennifer's never giving us a hard time again."

Jennifer, Alyssa, and Danielle stand in a circle, hands on hips, backpacks slung over shoulders. Danielle's swiping on lip gloss.

"Hi, Jennifer," I call.

Jennifer glances up at the sound of her name. Red flushes her neck and spreads to her face. Not an attractive look for her.

The girls ignore us as we walk past on our way to first period. I wonder how Jennifer explained to them that we're not targets anymore. I'm sure she didn't show them our video.

Shirlee high-fives me. "See you at lunch," she says, smiling.

The morning's kind of weird. All my teachers say the same thing: Way to go, Raine. Make sure you get caught up on your homework. Although Señor Lopez says it in Spanish, so maybe he told me I have an automatic A and can slack off for the rest of the year.

At lunch, Torie directs everyone where to sit and puts me in the middle.

"This is so not necessary," I say, sliding along the bench.

"We all have questions. If you're in the middle, everyone can hear you." She could go far in a career that requires extreme bossiness.

"It's incredible that you got evidence on the arsonist," Sydney says. "The police didn't even know his identity."

"That was Emily, not me." I unwrap my sandwich. "She figured out it was Michael White, got the evidence, knew about the cabin fire."

"You're the one who found Emily," Willow says.

I nod, taking a bite of my sandwich. I'm not okay with people thinking I'm a big hero when I'm not.

"Yeah, about that. How did it take you so long to notice Emily was living in your basement?" Torie asks.

Willow shoots her a look.

"She was quiet?" I shrug. "Seriously, I never go down

there. And it's one of those things you don't expect to happen. I mean, when was the last time you looked to see if someone was camped out in your basement?"

"Makes total sense," Willow says.

Everyone launches in about what they would've done, how often they go in the basement, how hard they sleep at night. Shirlee joins the table. I eat my sandwich. Then I end up describing the shed, Michael, the hospital, Emily.

"Are you on house arrest for life?" Sydney looks up from her soup. "My mom said if I tried anything like that, she'd never let me walk out the front door again."

"My mom was pretty irked. But she was also relieved I was, uh, alive," I say. Actually, it's the most I've ever seen my mom cry. She's still bursting into tears at odd moments, like when I'm feeding Levi or when I'm doing homework. "No, I'm not grounded. I've never been grounded. My mom doesn't really do that."

"How about Jennifer, Alyssa, and Danielle?" Willow asks. "Are they grounded?"

"No idea." I peel back the lid of my yogurt.

"They're doing a ton of community service," Shirlee says. "Probably till they're in their thirties."

"And we're getting an assembly on bullying. Whoo-hoo," Sydney says sarcastically.

"Why didn't you dial nine-one-one the minute you knew Michael took Emily?" Torie asks. "It would've been so much safer."

"Do you ever think before you open your mouth? Did

236

you see that?" Willow blinks excitedly. "I said a not-nice thing."

"It's fine." I wave away Willow's concerns. "Looking back, yeah, I probably should've. But I didn't know for sure he'd taken her to the woods. And the police didn't know Emily was still alive, so they would've asked a lot of questions. The other time I wish I'd called nine-one-one was when I found Michael's car. I probably had cell service at that point, and I lost it once I climbed the hill. Basically, I just did what I thought was the right thing at that moment."

By the end of lunch, I'm exhausted from being the center of attention. Plus I'm hungry, because with all the talking, I didn't finish eating.

Torie catches up to me and Shirlee on our way out of the cafeteria. "Did you hear why Hugh and Avalon broke up?" Torie asks. Before we have a chance to say anything, she answers her own question. "Avalon cheated on him."

"That's terrible," Shirlee says.

"Go after him now, Raine," Torie says. "The timing's perfect."

"I've been telling you your horoscope predicts romance," Shirlee says after Torie skips ahead to inform more people.

My afternoon teachers say the same things to me as the morning teachers. After film, I find our coach already on the track while everyone's still changing for practice in the locker room.

"Hi, Coach," I say.

"You doing okay, Raine?" He unwinds his whistle from around the clipboard and loops it over his head.

"I'm really sorry about the season."

"Yeah, well, the doctor said you're definitely out of commission?"

"No running for six months, but I should have a total recovery."

"That'll be good for the high school team." He looks at me. "You available to help at practices and events?"

"Definitely."

"I'm gonna move Willow up to varsity. Maybe you can work with her. Get her in the best possible shape for the first event."

"I can do that." Willow will be thrilled.

"And I'm putting you in charge of stats." He hands me a clipboard with my name written in black Sharpie on the back. "And water."

"Okay."

"Next time, don't take chances like that." He pats my shoulder a couple of times. "I'm glad you're okay."

Can you say *awkward*?

CHAPTER 34

*J*ustin, Hugh's older brother, looks a lot like Hugh, only taller and broader.

"So you're the one who caught Michael White?" he says, shooting a glance at me in the passenger seat.

"Emily Huvar deserves all the credit," I say for the millionth time. There's a sparkle on the dash and one on Justin's shirt. I shove my hands in my jeans pockets.

"I was in computer class with them last year." Justin backs down our driveway.

"What were they like?" Hugh asks from the backseat, where he's sitting next to our fake eighth grader. While I was in the hospital, Hugh cut a life-size guy out of cardboard and drew on eyes and hair and clothing. Interestingly, the cardboard cutout has a sparkle on his head.

"I never saw them talking to other people. Not even to each other," Justin says. "I don't think they were friends or anything."

"They weren't," I say, positioning myself so I can see Justin, Hugh, and Typical Yielding Teen at the same time.

"They both knew way more about computer science than the rest of us." Justin turns the corner.

Typical Yielding Teen flops over on Hugh. "I should've buckled this guy in," he says.

"You should've left him at home," Justin says.

"You don't think that, do you?" Hugh asks me. "We'll be the only group to have a fake student in their video."

"I can believe that." I'm actually starting to warm up to the idea.

"Extra credit," Hugh promises. "In the bag."

"Extra credit is good," I say. "What about the guy whose family owned the cabin?" I ask Justin. It's interesting to hear his take.

"Brandon Ford," Justin says. "On our football team. Good player, but maybe not the nicest guy. He's kind of aggressive. He lives on the same street as Michael."

"They live on the same street?" After all the conversations I've had with the police and all the articles online and all the news reports, you would think I'd know this.

"Yup. They've known each other forever. Brandon's a

jock. Michael's a nerd. It's your typical jock-makes-fun-of-nerd scenario." Justin switches lanes. "But I never saw it as a big deal. Not big enough to burn down the family cabin, anyway."

People might say that about how Jennifer treated me. But it was a big deal.

Justin speeds up on the ramp to the highway, and Typical Yielding Teen falls on Hugh again.

"You did that on purpose," Hugh says. "You're trying to give me paper cuts on my face."

"Yeah, right," Justin says, his lips twitching. "I'm trying to be a safe driver and accelerate to the speed of the highway traffic."

When I see brothers or sisters joking around like this, it makes me wish a little for a sibling.

We pass the shirt factory and an industrial park. Eventually, we exit the highway, and Justin swings into a parking lot and coasts to a spot in front of Mario's: WHERE WE'RE AT HOME LETTING **YOU** BE THE CHEF.

"You guys have exactly one hour, or you're walking back." Justin puts the car into neutral. "I have plans with my girlfriend."

"Thanks for the ride." I push open my door.

"No prob. And, Raine, you seem like a sensible girl," Justin says. "Feel free to accidentally leave Flat Stanley's cousin at Mario's."

Before entering the restaurant, Hugh and I prop up

Typical Yielding Teen by the door and film him. Then Hugh holds the door open for me, which is slightly awkward, as he's balancing more than five feet of cardboard with his other arm.

Inside, it's cozy and warm. Wooden tables and chairs dot the room. There's a strong, delicious smell of garlic and freshly baked dough.

"Table for two?" the host asks.

"Make that three." With his free hand, Hugh pushes his hair up his forehead. It falls back down.

We end up at a small corner table. The host drags over an extra chair.

"It's a project for school," I explain.

The waiter arrives with a couple of globs of dough, a bowl of marinara sauce, a bowl of ranch dressing, and a ton of toppings.

Hugh looks at me, a question in his eyes.

"No," I say firmly. "Pizza for two is enough. I'll share with our friend."

"Should we name him?" Hugh presses the heel of his hand in his dough.

I shake my head. "I don't want to get too attached. He's going to end up in a Dumpster by the end of next week."

"I don't think so." Hugh looks fake-hurt.

I laugh. "How about TYT? It's less of a mouthful."

"I was thinking more along the lines of Conrad."

"Why Conrad?"

"You don't think he looks like a Conrad? Conrad the cougar?" Hugh says.

Conrad the cougar. Our school mascot has a name. I like that.

"Actually, I think he looks more like a first name *Card*," I say, "last name *Board*."

Hugh groans.

We knead and talk and film.

"I made another playlist," Hugh says. "Still trying to convince you the Oily Artichokes are a second-rate band."

"I'm pretty much over the Oily Artichokes," I say. Michael ruined them for me.

"Yes!" Hugh makes a victory fist in the air, dusting us both with flour.

After I flatten my dough and cover it with sauce and toppings, we film Conrad adding more pepperoni.

I'm not sure whether I like Hugh *that* way, and I can't tell if he likes me *that* way. I think I do. I think he does. But I like hanging out with him. And I want to know him better. That's enough for now.

The sparkle on Hugh's shoulder winks at me.

I gaze around the room. A sparkle glints on a woman's purse. Another sparkle shines from the shelf where the waiters pick up food. My fingertips are tingling, itching to explore and find the memories I'm not seeing.

Since that first day of kindergarten, I've spent my life covering up how I'm different. I shove my hands in my pockets to stop from reaching out for sparkles. I grab them on the sly, hoping not to be caught. I lie about how I know stuff.

But tonight, kicking back in a fun restaurant with great smells and a cute guy, I realize something has changed.

I was part of something big. I helped bring down a bad guy, a guy who wanted to hurt people. I helped stop the mean girl and her friends. I helped a girl get back with her family.

None of this would've happened without the sparkles.

Who knows why I got this gift. Who knows what I'm supposed to do with it. But whatever the sparkles have in store for me, I'm ready.

ACKNOWLEDGMENTS

Thank you to the usual suspects at Delacorte Press, especially my editor, Wendy Loggia, whose incredible smarts and patience guided this book on its very long and winding road to publication; Kate Gartner for a most beautiful and creepy cover; Krista Vitola for taking care of loads of details and sending the best emails; and Tricia Callahan, Annette Szlachta-McGinn, and Colleen Fellingham for the excellent copyediting.

Very special thanks to my generous and enthusiastic critique partners, Kathy Krevat and Kelly Hayes; to Sergeant Joe Bulkowski for helping with all matters police; Jon Schoonover for sharing his cross-country expertise; to Vicki Sutherland for the nursing and burn info; to Rachel Moritz for her insightful early read; to the Jardels for allowing me to house- and cat-sit in their quiet, get-lots-of-writing-done home; to Claire Summy and Jacklyn Jardel for talking plots while trapped in my car traveling to and from the dance studio; and to my family, who no doubt put up with a lot of writing craziness. Yes, Mark, this book is finally out the door! XO

Huge, huge hugs to Rachel Vater Coyne. I do not even want to contemplate how many hours we spent discussing this book. Thank you for believing . . . and believing . . . and believing.